ff

STORIES FROM THE BIBLE

*From the Garden of Eden
to the Promised Land*

Walter de la Mare

faber and faber
LONDON · BOSTON

First published in 1929
First published as a Faber Paperback 1977
First published in this shortened version 1987
by Faber and Faber Limited
3 Queen Square London WC1N 3AU

Printed in Great Britain by
Richard Clay Ltd Bungay Suffolk

British Library Cataloguing in Publication Data

De la Mare, Walter
Stories from the Bible: from the Garden of Eden to the Promised Land. –
2nd ed.
1. Bible stories, English – O.T.
I. Title. II. Ardizzone, Edward III. Bible. O.T.
English. Selections
221.9'505   BS551.2
ISBN 0-571-14946-4

To Fridy

other books for children by Walter de la Mare

COLLECTED RHYMES AND VERSES

PEACOCK PIE

COLLECTED STORIES FOR CHILDREN

ANIMAL STORIES

THE THREE ROYAL MONKEYS

TALES TOLD AGAIN

MOLLY WHUPPIE
Illustrated by Errol Le Cain

Contents

[7]

Introduction

The stories contained in this volume are versions of but a few of the narratives related in the first books of the Old Testament of the Bible, "that inestimable treasure which excelleth all the riches of the earth".

The Bible, it is said, is not being read nowadays so much as it used to be: while there *was* a time when, it is recorded, a load of hay would be paid gladly for the loan of a manuscript Testament for an hour a day. Wholly apart from the profound truth that "simple men of wit may be edified much to heavenly living by reading and knowing of the Old Testament", this statement, if true, implies a loss beyond measure to mind and heart, and particularly to the young—its wisdom and divination, truth and candour, simplicity and directness. All that man is or feels or (in what concerns him closely) thinks; all that he loves or fears or delights in, grieves for, desires and aspires to is to be found in it, either expressed or implied. As for beauty, though this was not its aim, and the word is not often used in it—it is "excellent in beauty"; and poetry dwells in it as light dwells upon a mountain and on the moss in the crevices of its rocks. In what other book—by mere mention of them—are even natural objects made in the imagination so whole and fair; its stars, its well-springs, its war-horse, its almond tree?

That there are difficulties for those unfamiliar with its pages no one with any knowledge of the subject would deny. The very simplicity and austerity of the Old Testament stories, their conciseness, the slight changes that have occurred in the meaning or bearing of English words, occasional obscurities and repetitions in the text, are among them. My small endeavour has been to lighten some of these difficulties, while yet keeping as close to the spirit of the text as I am capable of. In many passages I have kept even to the letter. Apart from that, remembrance of what the matchless originals in the Bible itself meant to me when I was a child is still fresh and vivid in mind, and these renderings are little more than an attempt to put that remembrance as completely as I can into words.

But words in their influence are subtle and delicate beyond all things known to man, and the least change in them when they are in company, or the least addition to that company, cannot but entail a change of meaning; a change, that is, in their complete effect on the mind and spirit of the reader. Comparison of some of the English translations, as they deal in turn with the same brief passage, will be evidence of this, however little evidence is needed.

Here, for example, are three familiar verses from the first chapter of the Book of Ruth. Having come to the parting of the ways, Naomi, wholly against her heart and will, entreats Ruth to return to her own people and venture no further into a strange land:

"The which answerde, Ne contrarye thou me, that Y forsake thee, and goo a wey; whider euere thou gost, I shal goo, and where thow abidist, and I togidre shal abyde; thi puple my puple, and thi God my God; what erthe the takith diynge, in it I shal die, and there I shal take place of biriynge; thes thingis God do to me, and thes thingis adde, if not oonly deth me and thee seuere. Seynge thanne Noemye, that with stedfast inwit Ruth hadde demed to goo with hir, wold not contrarye, ne more mouynge the turnynge agen to hyrs. And thei wenten forth to gidre, and thei camen into Bethlem . . ."   (Wycliffe: *c.* 1382)

"And sche answeride, Be thou not aduersarye to me, that Y forsake thee, and go awei; whidur euer thou schalt go, Y shal go, and where thou schalt dwelle, and Y schall dwelle togidere; thi puple is my puple, and thi God is my God; what lond schal resseyue thee diynge, Y schal die ther ynne, and there Y schal take place of biriyng; God do to me these thingis, and adde these thingis, if deeth aloone schal not departe me and thee. Therfor Noemy saw, that Ruth hadde demyde with stidefast soule to go with hir, and sche nolde be agens hir, nether counseile ferthere turnynge agen to her cuntrei men. And thei geden forth togidere, and camen in to Betheleem . . ."

(The "Wycliffe" translation revised by
John Purvey: 1386)

"Ruth answered: Speake not to me thereof, that I shulde forsake thee, and turne backe from the: whither so euer thou goest, thither wil I go also: and loke where thou abydest, there wil I abide also: Thy people is my people, and thy God is my God. Loke where thou diest, there wil I dye, and euen there wil I also be buried. The Lorde do this and that unto me, death onely shal departe vs.

"Now whan she sawe, that she was stedfastly mynded to go with her, she spake nomore to her therof. So they wente on both together, till they came vnto Bethleem."

(Miles Coverdale: 1536)

"And Ruth answered, Intreate mee not to leaue thee, nor to depart from thee: for whither thou goest, I will goe: and where thou dwellest, I will dwell: thy people shalbe my people, and thy God my God. Where thou diest, will I die, and there will I be buried. The Lord do so to me and more also, if ought but death depart thee and me.

"When she saw yt she was stedfastly minded to goe with her, shee left speaking vnto her. So they went both vntill they came to Beth-lehem . . ."   (The Geneva Bible: 1560)

"She answered: Be not against me, to desire that I should leave thee and depart: for whithersoever thou shalt go, I will go: and where thou shalt dwell, I also will dwell. Thy people shall be my people, and thy God my God. The land that shall receive thee dying, in the same will I die; and there will I be buried. The Lord do so and so to me, and add more also, if aught but death part me and thee.

"Then Noemi seeing, that Ruth was steadfastly deter-mined to go with her, would not be against it, nor persuade her any more to return to her friends: So they went together and came to Bethlehem."   (The Douai Bible: 1609)

"And Ruth said, Entreat me not to leave thee, or to re-turn from following after thee: for whither thou goest, I will go: and where thou lodgest, I will lodge: thy people shall be my people, and thy God my God: Where thou diest, will I die, and there will I be buried: the Lord do so to me, and more also, if ought but death part thee and me.

"When she saw that she was stedfastly minded to go with her, then she left speaking unto her. So they went until they came to Bethlehem . . ."   (Authorized Version: 1611)

It is a lesson in much more than mere word-craft to con-sider each of these in turn. In one, the lovely simplicity of "that I forsake thee, and go away"; in another, "that Ruth had deemed with steadfast soul to go with her"; in another, "She spake no more to her thereof. So they went on both together"; and then, the sovran "Intreat me not to leave thee", and "the Lord do so to me and more also"; and last, in the Douai translation, "if aught but death part me and thee".

Here also is but a fragment from the second chapter of Genesis:

"And the Lord God brought forthe of the erthe eche tree fayre in sight, and swete to ete."   (Wycliffe)

"And the Lorde God caused to sprynge out of the earth all maner trees, pleasant to loke upon, and good to eate."

(Miles Coverdale: 1536)

"For out of the ground made the Lorde God to grow euery tree pleasant to the sight and good for meate."

(The Geneva Bible: 1560)

"And the Lord God brought forth of the ground all manner of trees, fair to behold and pleasant to eat of."

(The Douai Bible: 1609)

"And out of the ground made the Lord God to grow every tree that is pleasant to the sight and good for food."

(Authorized Version: 1611)

If these are the varying achievements of the masters, what manifold dangers, then, await the "simple creature" who attempts in our own day to re-tell even a fraction of any particular chapter of the Old Testament in his own words.

To read, too, any book worthy of the name needs all the powers of understanding and imagination and spirit of which one is capable, and even then, what is made of the reading may fall far short of what was intended in the writing. How much so, then, when that book is the Bible! Its unique history is proof of it. Even the most usual of words in the most ordinary of circumstances may have many senses. We say, "Here I am, at home": meaning, "in my own familiar place": and, maybe, "the house where I was born". But as when striking a note softly on a piece of fine glass one may listen on to its chiming overtones, so, if we listen to the echoes of the word home in memory, they can hardly fail to remind us of the home that is the body, where the "I, myself", has its earthly dwelling. Next, maybe, of the "keeping in order" of that home. And last, of the home of the heart's desire, which has had almost as many names given to it as there are races of mankind.

"Worde," as Wycliffe says, "worde wynd and mannes mynd is full short, but letter written dwelleth." So too with the Bible. Its meanings or "understandings", as St. Thomas Aquinas declared, are fourfold. First the literal, which is "ground and foundement" of the other three—the allegorical, the moral and the analogical.

These words sound a little formidable, but no word is "long", when one knows the meaning of it. Thus the word Jerusalem may mean first, literally, the chief city of Palestine—seated beyond the barren hills between it and the sea, and of an age-long, unique and tragic history. Next, allegorically, it may signify also the Jerusalem that is the longed-for Zion, the place of peace, the Church on earth. Next, morally, it may signify the soul of man. And last, analogically, in what by retention it resembles, it is the place of paradise, "where there shall be bliss in body and soul without end". The Jerusalem of King David, that is; the Jerusalem of Christ, the Messiah; the Jerusalem mourned and desired in every human heart; the heavenly Jerusalem otherwhere. Or again, the literal refers to things that happen or have happened on earth, the allegorical to what is to be believed, the moral to what is to be done, and the analogical to what is to be hoped for in the life to come.

A word in the Old Testament in the inspiration of the man who wrote it, may be taken to bear only one of these interpretations, or more than one, or all. So, too, in differing respects, in other writings. William Blake's "Tiger", for example; is it to read too much into his poem if we see in it the tiger that ranges the forest of the night, the tiger that is the emblem of strength and ferocity, the tiger that is the exemplar of fearlessness, the tiger that is a revelation of the miracle of divine creativeness? And so, too, maybe, when Shakespeare wrote of "what we fear of death". But here I am venturing beyond my depth.

All this, at least, concerns the stories contained in this volume as they appear, once and for all, in the all-sufficing "bare text" of the Old Testament itself. My own versions of them, apart from what has been literally embodied from it (and even here the frame given to that must in some degree affect its meaning), is no more than my own conception of them, which cannot but be very partial, faulty, inaccurate, and far from complete.

Little evidence though there may be of it, and however inadequately I have taken advantage of their learning and insight, I am indebted to many authorities and commentators, though it would be only the poorest of tributes to specify them. My deepest thanks, however, may be expressed to friends who have generously helped me, to Sister Frances de Chantal for invaluable kindness and counsel, to Mr. Forrest Reid and to Mr. R. N. Green-Armytage for their kindness in reading and commenting on my proofs. Nevertheless the full responsibility for what is here—and I realize how serious a responsibility it is—cannot but remain entirely my own.

If, in spite of all its defects and shortcomings, this book persuades any of its young readers to return to the inexhaustible well-spring from which it came, it will have amply fulfilled its purpose.

THE GARDEN
OF EDEN

The Creation of Man

I n the beginning the Lord God created the heaven and
the earth. And the earth was without form, and void.
All was darkness, confusion and watery chaos. But the
spirit of the Lord God, in whose sight a thousand years
are but as yesterday, brooded in divine creation upon the

dark face of the waters. And God said: "Let there be light." And there was light. And God saw the light, that it was good.

And he divided the wondrous light called Day from the darkness that he called Night. And he parted asunder the waters of the firmament called heaven from the waters beneath upon the earth. And the dry land appeared, its desolate plains and drear ice-capped mountains. And he made the green seeding grass to grow, and herb and tree yielding fruit; and he saw that it was good.

In the heaven above, for sign of the seasons and of days and of years, and to divide the day from the night, he set the sun and the moon to shine and to lighten the whole earth. The sun, the greater light, ruled the day, and the moon, the lesser light, that waxes and wanes in radiance ever changing, ruled the night; and the wandering planets had each its circuit in heaven, and the stars their stations in the depth and height of space.

Then said the Lord God: "Let the waters bring forth abundantly moving creatures that have life, and winged birds of the air that may fly above the earth under the firmament of heaven." So there were fishes in the deep sea, and great whales had their habitation therein, and the air was sweet with birds.

And when the heavens and the earth and all the host of them were finished in the days that the Lord God appointed, he for ever blessed and hallowed the seventh day, because in joy and love he had stayed then and rested from all his work which he had created and made.

Of the power and wisdom of God was everything to which he had given life—tree and plant and flower and herb, from the towering cedar to the branching moss. All the beasts of the earth also, the fishes of the sea, the fowls of the air, the creeping things and the insects, each in the place where was its natural food and what was needful for its strength and ways and wants; from beasts so mighty and ponderous that they shook the ground with their tread, to the grasshopper shrilling in the sunshine on his blade of grass and the silent lovely butterfly sipping her nectar in the flower; from the eagle in the height of the skies to the wren flitting from thicket to thicket, each after its own kind.

The Lord God saw everything that he had made, and behold, it was very good. He blessed it, and bade all things living grow and increase and multiply upon the earth, wheresoever it was meet for them. But still in his power and wisdom he was not satisfied with the earth that he had created until, last of all things living, he made man. And he called him by name, Adam.

For dwelling-place meet for this man that he had made the Lord God planted a garden. It was a paradise of all delight, wherein he intended him to have bliss in body and soul without end. And though it was of the earth, it was yet of a beauty and peace celestial, wherein even the angels of heaven might find joy to stray.

This garden lay eastward in Eden; and a river went out of Eden to water it. Flowing thence, and beyond it, its waters were divided, and they became the four great rivers of the world, whose names have been many.

The name of the first river was Pison, which flows about and encompasses the whole land of Havilah, where there is gold. And the gold of that land is fine gold. There also is found the gum of spicery called bdellium, sweet to the taste and bitter to the tongue, and the clear green onyx or beryl stone. The name of the second river was Gihon, whose windings encompass the whole land of Ethiopia. And the name of the third river was Hiddekel, or Tigris, that flows eastward of the land Assyria. And the fourth great river of the world is the Euphrates.

But by any device of knowledge, desire, or labour, to return from beyond Eden by any one of these rivers into that Garden is now for man a thing impossible. Its earthly paradise is no more.

Then, every beast and living thing that was in the Garden, and roved its shades and valleys and drank of its waters, was at peace in the life that had been given it, without fear or disquietude or wrong. But as yet they had no names. Trees grew in abundance on the hills and in the valleys of the Garden, and every tree that sprang forth out of the earth was fair in sight and good to eat.

In the crystal waters of its river swam fish curious and marvellous in scale and fin and in their swift motion in the water; and flowers of every shape and hue grew so close in company upon its banks that the air was coloured with the light cast back from their clear loveliness. The faintest breeze that stirred was burdened with their fragrance. And at certain seasons a mist went up out of the Garden; and night-tide shed its dews, watering the whole face of the ground, refreshing all things.

And in the very midst of the Garden were two trees, secret and wondrous; the Tree of Life, and the Tree of the Knowledge of Good and Evil. Their branches rose in a silence so profound that no cry of bird or beast was heard there, and no living thing shaped by the Lord God out of the dust of the earth ever drew near.

Now the man whom the Lord God had created was different from every other living thing upon the earth. Miraculous in grace and life and strength, his lighted eyes, his hair, his hands, the motion of his limbs, the mystery of his beating heart, his senses to touch and taste and smell and

hear and see—miraculous also in the wonder of his mind
that reflected in little all things of the great world around
him—he too, like all else that had life in the Garden, had
been fashioned and shaped of the dust. Yet was he in the
image and likeness of the divine; the Lord God had
breathed into him breath of life, and he became a living
soul.

Since his body, like theirs, was also of the earth, Adam
was at peace with all living creatures in the Garden. Nevertheless because in mind and spirit he was man and no beast,
God made him the lord and master of the Garden, sove-
reign even to the fishes of the water, to the birds of heaven
and the unreasonable beasts of earth. He had dominion
over them all. And as the free and harmless creatures that
for a happy dwelling-place shared the Garden with him
were less than he, so he himself was a little lower than the
angels of heaven, who are not of the earth, but of a different
being and nature, and dwell in glory beyond thought or
imagination in the presence of the Lord God.

Thus Adam, shaped of the dust and given life of the
divine, came into this earthly paradise, and his eyes were
opened, and the light of day shone in upon him as through
windows, and joy and amazement filled his mind. He heard
the voice of beast and bird and wind and water, and with
his fingers he touched the flowers. He was clothed in the
light and heat of the sun, and stood erect and moved his
limbs and stretched his arms above his head. The Lord God
looked on him with love and talked with him in the secrecy
of his heart.

"Lo, all things that I have made to be of thy company I
give into thy charge to keep and tend and to use. Do with
them as thy heart desires. And behold, I have given thee
also for food every herb whose seed is in itself of its own

kind, and every tree yielding fruit and seed. Of every tree thou mayest freely eat except only the fruit of the Tree of the Knowledge of Good and Evil that is in the midst of the Garden. Of that thou mayest not eat. It is denied thee. For if thou eat of it, it will bring thee only grief and misery; deadly of its nature is this fruit unto thee, and in the day that thou eatest thereof thou shalt surely die."

Adam hearkened to these words with all his understanding, and in the will of the Lord God he found freedom and his peace. The days of his life went by, and the Lord God brought to him in his own season every beast of the field and every fowl of the air that he had made out of the dust, to see what Adam would call it, and to see which of them was most meet to him for company. And Adam gazed at them, marvelling as they moved before him, each in its own kind following the instinct and desire that was the secret of its life.

And as Adam watched them, it seemed that of his own insight and divination he shared in the life and being of each one of them in turn. They wandered amid the branching trees, browsing in the herbage, and on the gentle slopes at the river's brink stooped their heads to quench their thirst, or stretched themselves to drowse in the sunshine, or lay cleaning and preening their sleek coats, or sported in play one with another, and leaped and exulted.

Adam watched too the birds among the green-leafed branches, and the prudent and loving ways of the water-fowl. The swan with plumage markless as the snow was there, and the goose on high at evening arrowed the still air, winging in company of her kind. In the hush of dark the little owl called *a-whoo* into the warm silence, and the nightingale sang on whether the moon shone in the dark or no, though all through the day it had been singing too.

Adam listened, never wearying of their cries and songs. And whatsoever—according to the exclamations of wonder, surprise or delight that came to his lips at sight or hearing of them—Adam called them, such were their names. To every living thing he gave a name. Its image and its name were of one memory in his mind. At call of its name the creature to whom he had given it came fearlessly to his side. He rejoiced to see it, and at sound of his laughter the Garden itself seemed also to rejoice and to renew its life.

At evenfall the Lord God would return into the Garden and talk with Adam, communing with him in the secrecy of his heart. And even when Adam slept, his divine presence haunted him in dreams, and when he awoke to day again his love enfolded him. As naturally as the birds in their singing, Adam praised the Lord God in all that he did.

But though he had joy in the company of the creatures around him in the Garden, Adam had none like to himself with whom to share his own spirit and nature. He was in this apart from them and was alone. And the Lord God read this secret in Adam's heart and had compassion on his solitude.

"It is not good," he said, "that the man whom I have created should be alone; I will make him a help meet for him."

In the darkness of night he caused a deep sleep or trance to fall upon Adam, and out of his side as he slept he took a rib, and with a touch closed again and healed the wounded side. And as he had made all things living and Adam himself out of the dust, so in the mystery of his wisdom he made woman out of man. He breathed into her body the breath of life, and in the stillness of night she lay, as yet unawakened, beside Adam as he slept.

When daybreak lightened again over Eden and the shafts

of sunrise pierced its eastern skies, the voice of the bird of morning stole sweet and wildly in upon Adam's dreams, and the very rocks resounded. He awoke, and saw the woman. She lay quiet as a stone, the gold of the sun mingling with the gold of her hair, her countenance calm and marvellous.

Adam stooped in awe and wonder and with his finger touched her hand, as in the beginning the Lord God had with his divine touch bidden him rise and live. So too the woman's eyes opened and looked upon Adam, and out of one paradise he gazed into another. And love breathed in him, seeing that she was of his own form and likeness. As he looked upon her, he cried with joy: "This, this is now bone of my bones and flesh of my flesh!"

So Adam was no longer alone in the Garden. She whom he called woman because she had been created by the Lord God out of man, was his continual company and delight. She was Eve, Adam's wife. They two were one, and this is the reason why a man, leaving even his father and his mother, cleaves to his wife. And in the paradise of earth and mind which had been made for them, Adam and Eve were both of them naked, for they were of all innocence as are children, and they were not ashamed.

Happy and at peace together beyond the heart of man now to dream of or conceive, Adam and Eve dwelt in the Garden of Eden, tending and dressing it to keep it fair and well.

The Fall from Grace

Now of all living creatures in Eden the serpent was more subtle than any other which the Lord God had made. And because of his subtlety there entered into him the knowledge and malice of an angel fallen because of pride from grace, and banished from the presence of the Lord God. This fallen angel's evil influence found harbourage within the serpent; and Adam knew it not.

Couched in his beauty upon his coils, cold and stealthy, the changing colour of his scales rippling his whole length through, the serpent with lifted head would of his subtlety seek their company and share with them a knowledge that was his only. He would drowse beside them in the sun's heat while they talked together, and as he listened, envy sprang up in him, and he hated them for their innocence and their peace in their happy obedience to him who had made them and set them free.

There came an hour in the fullness of morning when Adam was away from the woman, and the serpent, seeing it, approached her and was with Eve alone. She sat in dappled shade from the sun, whose light was on all around them, and whose heat was pleasant to her after the cold of the waters in which she had bathed. There she had seen her own image or reflex in its glass; and she had praised the Lord God at the thought she was so fair. The serpent lifted up his flat-browed head, fixed his eyes upon her as she sat sleeking her hair, and he said: "Where, now, is the man Adam?"

Eve told the serpent that he was gone into the glades of the Garden near at hand to gather fruit for them to eat.

The serpent couched lower, rimpling the scales upon his skin. "But is it not", he said, "that the Lord God hath forbidden thee and the man Adam, saying, 'You shall not eat of any of the trees in the Garden'?"

Eve smiled, marvelling that the serpent should so speak.

"Nay," she said, "we may eat of the fruit of any of the trees in the Garden. Except only the fruit of the Tree that is in the midst of it. Of that the Lord God hath said: 'You shall not eat of it. Taste it not lest you die!'"

The Garden was still. Above them the wondrous blue of morning was brimmed with the light of day, and the shadows of tree and mountain moved with the sun. Except for the warbling of birds, there came no sound of any other voice between them, and the serpent drew back his head, and from his cold and changeless eyes steadfastly looked upon Eve, loveliest of all things on earth that the Lord God had made.

"Yea," he answered, "and so the Lord God has said! But of a surety thou shalt not die. For he himself knows well that in the day that thou eat of the fruit of this Tree, then shall thine eyes be opened to his wisdom and thou shalt be as the divine ones, the angels of heaven, knowing both good and evil. It is no wonder that the fruit of the Tree hath been forbidden thee, for even though thou share it not with me, thou hast thine own secret wisdom. I did but desire to show thee how sweet and delectable are the fruits that grow upon this strange Tree's branches."

Eve listened to the guile of the serpent. She stooped her head upon her shoulders and thought deeply within herself of what he had said. And the serpent watching her, held his peace.

At length she answered him. "I know not", she said, "where grows the Tree. And Adam my husband expressly told me not even to seek to look upon it unless he were with me. It is well that the Lord God hath forbidden us the Tree, if only evil come of it."

"Yea," said the serpent. "But verily Adam thy husband hath seen it. I know well where grows this Tree of Knowledge. Come, now, let us go together, and thou thyself shalt see with thine own eyes how harmless it is. Yea, verily, it far surpasses every other tree that is in the Garden; and when I myself quaffed in its fragrance there was none to say me nay. But it may be thou hast no thirst for this wisdom, and thy husband himself would keep it from thee."

The woman rose with trembling hands and looked hither and thither, seeking Adam. But in vain, and the serpent was already gone from her. With a faint cry she followed after him, and the serpent went on before her.

The way became strange to her. It narrowed in beneath lofty trees whose upper branches, interlacing their leaves together under the noon, shut out the day. The ground rose steeply, crag and boulder, but smooth with moss and pleasant to the foot. They descended into a ravine where streams of water brawled among rocks, meeting to part again. Birds of smouldering and fiery plumage, so small they seemed to be of flame, and butterflies, with damasked wings, hovered over the wide-brimmed flowers.

But soon these were few and showed no more. And there were now no birds or any living thing, and in silence they continued on their way ever going up now through the secret places of the Garden, and hidden in a shade so deep no star of night could pierce it, or the moon shine in. The air was cold as water from a well, and there was not even sighing of wind in the midst of the forest to cool Eve's cheek. But it seemed to her that she heard the music of voices afar off and as it were out of the midst of the morning, between the earth and the firmament.

She stayed her steps to listen. And the serpent tarried beside her while she rested, for she was weary with the steepness of the way. Her eyes entreated him, for her mind was troubled, but speech was over between them, and she followed again after him, to discover whence the music of the voices she heard was sounding.

They came out from the verge and shade of the forest into a hollow space of a marvellous verdure that fell away, then rose in slope towards a mountain that towered high beyond it, transfigured with a light that seemed too rare and radiant to be only the light of day. On either side of this mountain, its rocks illumined with the colours of their own bright stone and of the multitudinous flowers that mantled over them, Eve gazed into the vacancy of space. It was as though they had come to the earth's end.

And midway on the green of the mountain slope there was a Tree, the Tree of the Knowledge of Good and Evil, while above it, but well-nigh invisible in the light that dwelt upon it, there was another Tree, and that on the heights beyond.

The sounds as of voices and instruments of music faint and far, and of the rapture of thousands upon thousands beyond telling, had ceased; and it was as though the radiant blue were agaze with the eyes of a great multitude, lost to vision in the light of heaven.

"Lo, now," the serpent whispered in Eve's ear, "methought I heard the sound of voices, but all is still, and there is none to watch or hear us."

And Eve approached and drew near to the Tree, whose branches as of crystal shone in the light of day, ravishing her eyes. Buds and petalled flowers lay open upon them, and they were burdened also with their fruit, both ripening and ripe. A nectar-like fragrance lay upon the air, and the Tree was of a beauty and strangeness that made her heart pine within her.

And behold, the fruit that was upon the Tree seemed sweet and pleasant and desirable to the sight, a fruit to make one wise. Eve looked upon it, and thirsted, though a voice in her own mind called in warning to her of the deathly and infinite danger she was in. And though she remembered the words of Adam that the Lord God had spoken, yet she heeded them not.

The eyes of the serpent were fixed upon her, stealthy with malice, and an envy came upon her senses. She put out her hand and plucked one of the fruits that hung low upon the Tree, and raised it to her lips. Its odour filled her with desire of it. She tasted and did eat, and shuddering at its potency that coursed into her veins, she stayed without motion and as if in sleep.

With her long gentle hand she drew back her hair that lay heavy as gold upon her shoulders, and supple as the serpent himself languished in her own beauty. She raised her head and stared with her eyes, exulting and defiant, yet the radiance of the mountain now smote upon her eyes and dazzled her mind not as with light but with darkness. Dread and astonishment came upon her, and in fear even of herself she turned for help to the serpent that had persuaded her there with his false and evil counsel. And behold, she was alone. She was alone and knew herself for-

saken. With the fruit that she had plucked from the forbidden branches she drew back cowering from beneath the
Tree; and she fled away.

The darkness of the forest smote cold upon her body as
she fled on by the way she had come, stumbling and falling
and rising again, seeking she knew not what, but only to
escape from the wild tumult of her mind. Her naked limbs
bruised, her breath spent, she came into the presence of

Adam her husband who had come forth to seek her. With countenance bleak and strange, she crouched kneeling before him, thrust the fruit into his hand, and said: "See, see, the wonder the serpent hath made known to us! Taste and see!"

Her voice rang falsely on his ear. At sight of her face he trembled and, utterly loth and because he loved her, he took the fruit, and deaf to the voice within him, did eat.

In that moment they knew that they had sinned. Their eyes were opened; they looked out upon the Garden, and all things that were familiar in it were now become estranged and remote from them. Power was in their minds, but of knowledge, not of love. A grief no speech could reveal had veiled its beauty. In fear and horror they gazed on one another. Shame overshadowed them. They saw that they were naked, yet knew not where to turn to hide from their own shame. They plucked off leaves from a fig-tree and sewing them together made themselves aprons.

Smitten with doubt, they turned away each from each, and the love that was between them faded from out of their faces like the dew that vanishes in the heat of the day. Burning, mute, shaken with fear, yet on fire with life, they sat, their minds in torment; then, not daring to raise their horror-stricken eyes to sight, they turned again as if for refuge one to another. And Eve hid her face in Adam's hands, and they wept.

At sound of it a fawn that was browsing in a green hollow beneath the branches of a cedar tree lifted its eyes towards them, and, as if in fear, sped away and fled.

Night drew near; the level rays of the sun barred with shadow the vale in which they sat, and the milk-white flowers at their feet were dyed with its red. The firmament above them was flooded as if with flame, that as they looked ebbed out and was quenched. And the song of a multitude

[33]

of birds in their green haunts rose to a wild babbling rapture that now was desolation to them to hear, then died away and all was stilled.

And behold the serpent was of their company. "Hail, wise and happy!" he whispered with flickering tongue.

But even as they gazed on him with horror and loathing in their eyes, they heard in the silence the sound of the Lord God walking in the Garden in the cool of the day, in the sweet fresh air that comes with evening. They were sore afraid, and hid themselves from his presence amongst the trees of the Garden. But even as they stood together, seeking in vain for refuge where none could be, there came the voice of the Lord calling to Adam.

"Adam, where art thou?"

And the sound of the voice that had been their life and joy stilled their hearts with terror. They came forth from out of their hiding-place, and Adam bowed his head, for he dared not look upon the Lord God.

He said: "I heard thy voice in the Garden, and I was afraid, because I was naked; and I hid myself."

And the Lord God said: "Who told thee that thou wast naked? Hast thou then eaten of the fruit of the Tree, whereof I commanded thee that thou shouldst not eat?"

Adam bowed his head yet lower, hiding his face, his eyes fixed upon the ground.

"The woman", he said, "whom thou thyself gavest to be with me, she gave me of the Tree, and I did eat."

And the Lord God said unto the woman: "What is this that thou hast done?"

And the woman said, weeping: "The serpent beguiled me—and I did eat."

Then said the Lord God to the serpent: "Because thou hast done this thing, thou art from henceforth accursed among all living things upon the earth. Upon thy belly shalt thou crawl, both thou and thy kind, and dust shalt thou eat all the days of thy life, and all that come after thee. And I will put enmity between thee and the woman, and between thy seed, and all that shall spring out of thee, and her seed. And it shall bruise and crush thee, and thou shalt lie in wait to bruise her heel."

The serpent, the all-subtle one, the sower of mischief, sorrow and malice, looked stonily upon the Lord God, hearing his doom, in evil cold and corrupt. And this Satan went forth from out of his presence, eternal foe of man, though in the loving-kindness of the Lord God there should arise one to defeat his evil and to redeem man's sin, and paradise shall be restored to him again.

When the serpent was gone his way, the Lord God said to the woman: "Because of this that thou hast done, thy griefs shall be many. In sorrow and anguish thou shalt bring forth children. Yet the desire of thine own nature shall bind thee to thy husband. In him shall be thy strength and refuge, and he shall rule over thee."

And unto Adam he said: "Because thou hast hearkened to the voice of thy wife, and hast eaten of the Tree of which I commanded thee, saying, 'Thou shalt not eat of it,' cursed shall be the ground for thy sake and by reason of thy sin. Thorns also and thistles shall it bring forth, and weeds shall cumber thy labour, and thou shalt eat the green herb that springs therefrom. But in toil and in weariness and in the sweat of thy brow shalt thou find thy bread all the days of thy life, until thou lay down thy body in death, and be turned again into the earth whence thou wast taken. For dust thou art and unto dust shalt thou return."

And Adam and Eve, smitten to the soul, fled away from the presence of the Lord God into the night, and returned into the darkness of their hiding-place in the Garden. The Lord God was grieved to the heart because of their sin and sorrow, and communing in his wisdom he said within himself: "Behold, this man is become like unto one that is divine, seeing that, though it is not for his own peace, he hath attained the knowledge of good and evil. And now it may be in pride and disobedience he may sin yet again, and put forth his hand and pluck of the fruit of the Tree of Life, and eat and live for ever in shame and grief."

Therefore did the Lord God, though he was never to leave them utterly alone or abandon them, determine to cast Adam and Eve forth from out of the Garden of Eden, and to exile them into a world that could be no more a paradise, and where there could be no peace except that which their love and desire of him could bring them, for solace of their bitter banishment.

In the darkness that is before dawn they awoke where they lay, but into the sorrow where sleep had found them. They arose, and behold, there stood in watch round about them Cherubim of heaven whose eyes were like flames in the light of their countenances, unendurable to their gaze.

Adam and Eve fled from before them, stricken with dread, cold with anguish, and came through chasms to where in the sea-like gold of the risen sun the river of Eden flowed out beyond the Garden, falling in foam with sound of thunder from height to height. And the vast circuit of the earth lay spread out beneath them where they stood, dense with enormous forests, parched with sand, chequered with ice-capped mountains, through whose valleys the four rivers rolled their waters, which are the four great rivers of the world.

Thither they went down out of Eden, and dared not rest, until, looking back, even the verges of the Garden that had been their joy and peace were hidden from them. And night fell, cold and dark, and they were alone.

And at the east of the paradise whence God had cast out Adam, he set Cherubim, angels of heaven, and in their hands were flaming swords, turned every way, to keep and guard the way of the Tree of Life.

THE FLOOD

The Flood

Centuries of time went by, and the generations of man continually increased on the earth. They scattered over wider and wider tracts of country, venturing on into regions until then strange and untrodden. There were some who lived a life of continual roving and wandering. They pitched their tents in the wild as fancy led. Others found good pastures and dwelt there, tilling the ground and gathering together flocks of sheep and herds of cattle. Yet others reared up cities, and walled them in and fortified them against their foes. And they set up kings over them, mighty in pride and soldiery and armed with weapons of war.

They learned, too, the skill of many handicrafts and how to work in metals. They fashioned instruments of music, for dancing and feasting.

They made wine out of the grape and were merry. And the daughters of men were fair as the morning. They walked in their beauty like barbaric queens, bedecked with fine raiment and jewels of gold and coloured gems.

In these days men lived to a great age, and amassed knowledge and discovered secret arts and became practised in magic, and were wise in their own eyes.

But though there was no end to the skill and invention and curiosity of their minds, the spirit of life within them languished as if in a prison-house, and was darkened. The knowledge of what is good and what evil was theirs. They were free to make choice between them. They chose evil and not good, and refused the Lord God their love and obedience.

Pitiless and defiant, wherever they went, greed and violence and cruelty went with them, and no man was safe. They not only did evil, but in heart and imagination hated and fought against the good. The memory of the paradise that had been made for man had become less than the substance of a dream. And when, in despair at the defeat of their wild desires, its vision returned to them, they mocked it down and reviled the very thought of it. Angels fallen from grace entered in upon the earth in those days, and there were tyrants and giants in the land, terrible and mighty. Human life had become a mockery and a snare, because of the vileness of the spirit within.

And the Lord God, looking down from the heavens upon the earth which he had created, once radiant with light and peace and innocence, and now a waste of sin and woe, repented him that he had given life to the dust. He was grieved to the heart that man, whom he had made in his own image and of his divine love, had fallen to a state so dark that even the hope and desire of goodness had perished in him. And the Lord God said: "I will do away man, whom I made out of nought, from the face of the earth, and all things that have life; for it repenteth me that I created them."

One alone of all men living found grace in his eyes. He was faithful and blameless. Loving goodness and hating evil, he had withdrawn himself from his fellowmen and lived apart from them; and the Lord God was with him in the silence and secrecy of his heart. The name of this man was Noah, and he had three sons, Shem, Ham and Japheth.

There came a day when the Lord God warned Noah that an end was soon to come to the evil that man had brought upon the earth, and that it should be cleansed of its wickedness and corruption. And he bade Noah build an ark, or ship, directing him in the knowledge and understanding of his mind how in all things it should be made. As the Lord God bade him, so did Noah. He chose out and felled cypress and pine for timber, and with his three sons laboured day by day, until night came down and they went to rest, to fashion and build the ark, though as yet they knew neither its use nor its purpose. In length this ark was to be three hundred cubits—a hundred and fifty human paces from end to end. In breadth it was to be fifty cubits; and in height thirty—of such a height, that is, that the topmost branches of an oak tree would show green above its roof.

When Noah and his sons, having hewn and planed their timber, had laid the central keel and buttressed it and built up the curved ribs of the ark and roofed it with beams, they walled it all in with planks of cypress round about, shaping and leaving in it a narrow window, which skirted the whole circuit of the margin of the roof that covered it in. A great door also was made for its entering-in in the side of the ark, which could be opened and shut at need.

When this had been done and the towering outer walls or shell of the ark were sound and secure in all their joints and angles, they daubed them over with melted pitch or bitumen to make it proof against the weather and to seal up all crevices and crannies there might be between its timbers, so that no water could enter in.

That done, they built up within the ark and beneath its roof, three separate floors or storeys, with cross-pieces and planks, the lowermost in the belly or underpart of the ark, the other midway above it, and the third beneath the long narrow window that had been cut out within the space of eighteen inches from the margin of the roof. They left openings, too, or hatchways, at fitting intervals in each of the three floors or storeys, with a ladder to each by which those within the ark would be able to ascend and descend from one to the other.

These they then divided by walls into rooms or chambers of various shapes and sizes, convenient and proportionate, and all in accordance with the plan and design made by Noah. When these were complete with their doors and passage-ways, they daubed over the whole of the inside of the ark with pitch also.

For many months Noah and his three sons toiled on in the building of the ark, pausing only to eat and for rest and sleep. They chose out only the finest trees and perfect timber for their purpose and fashioned and finished their handiwork with all the skill they could.

But the day came at length when their work was at an end. The last wooden peg had been driven home, the last inch pitched, and all refuse had been cleansed away and removed. And lo! more gigantic in shape and bulk than any monster that had then its being in the depths of the oceans, their great ark, or ship—mastless and rudderless—lay ready. It was made, and in all things complete. Pitch-black and glistening in the splendour of the sun and high upon dry land it towered, in no way fine and delicate, but of immeasurable stoutness and stability, and strong to withstand not only the buffetings of wind and tempest, but to ride in safety upon waters wild as those of the sea.

They stood together in its shadow, looking up and surveying it, and they rejoiced at sight of it and at the thought that their anxious toil was over. That evening they feasted with their wives and their children, and gave thanks to the

Lord God; so that this day should always remain with them in mind and be held in solemn and happy remembrance.

When Noah and his three sons had finished the building of the ark, the word of the Lord God came again to Noah. He was warned that a great flood or deluge was soon to descend upon the earth, blotting out for ever in one swift death the evil and violence and cruelty of men without pity and without remorse.

But with Noah himself the Lord God made a covenant of peace. He promised him that he, with his wife and his sons and all his household, should be saved alive when that day of judgment should come. For this the ark had been made. Of all men living Noah alone had remained just and faithful.

As in the building of the ark, so in all things else that the Lord God bade him, Noah obeyed. And during the weeks that followed he himself and his three sons laboured without ceasing to prepare against the calamity that was soon to overwhelm the earth. For it was not only they themselves who were to find a place of refuge, but Noah had been bidden to assemble together two of every kind of living thing that was on the earth, beasts of the field and of the forest, birds of the air, and whatsoever around them enjoyed the breath of life.

To keep these creatures safe until the day when they should enter with them into the ark, Noah and his three sons made pens and folds, fencing them in so that no wild thing from without should enter, or captive within win free. They found caves also in the hills and rocks for beasts that are by nature wild and solitary in their habits, or secret and timid. When this was done, Noah's three sons went each his own way according as their father had directed them, to entice or snare or drive into the places prepared for them the living creatures they had in mind. From least to greatest they knew their ways and natures, and where to seek them, and how to tame and persuade them to submit themselves into their keeping, both the timorous and delicate and the fierce and strong.

So day by day and week by week they gathered together two of every kind of living thing that roved around them or dwelt beneath the blue of heaven in the sweet winds and rains and dews, throughout the region of valley, plain and mountain, lying in a wide circuit around the place wherein they had built the ark. Mate with mate they brought them in, and fed them and kept them secure and in good liking, lion and lioness, the fox and his vixen, horse and mare, bull and cow, ram and ewe, boar and sow, the wide-browed elephant and his mate, the gazelle and the hare, the coney of the sands, the antelope of the rocks, sheep and goat, the crafty cat, the gnawing rat, and the dark-delighting mouse. All these and countless others they assembled in the resorts that had been prepared for them, making ready for the day of the entering-in. The birds of the air, too, of every kind and feather, shape and song, from the eagle of noonday to the little wren—the gentle pelican, the blue-mooned peacock, the cuckoo and the thrush; all these and every living thing besides—where Noah and his sons had bestowed them, and in quarters best fitting for their ways and natures —awaited the day of the entering-in.

The ark was set in the midst, and busy continually was the whole household of Noah. Twilight descended; and they rested from their labours. The absent ones returned to the camp. The cries and callings of the four-footed creatures, and the birds' shrill sweet evensong ceased beneath the stars in the hush of the plain around them, where darkness enclosed them in. All was still.

And sleep enfolded them, renewing life and strength in

wayworn foot and weary limb. Only the nightingale poured on into the starry dark a song of delight, that yet seemed to echo with grief and exile.

Strangers sometimes came that way, men with their hunting-dogs—men of great stature and faced like the hawk; keen and ferocious. Noah greeted them with civility and offered them food and drink. But when he solemnly warned them of the horror and destruction that were soon to come upon the earth, they merely mocked at him. They surveyed with their hard bright eyes the great clumsy wooden ship that lay casting its vast shadow on the grass beside it in the light of the sun, then turned their heads and stared insolently into his face as if into that of a man without wits, or with a mind ridden by the haggard deceits of insanity.

They spurned his gifts, jeered at his warnings, and went their way, blinded in their folly even to the changes and strange appearances in the heavens and in the scene around them that were revealing themselves before their very eyes.

The weather darkened; winds wailing in the vacancy of space rose up and fell again. Vast flights of birds showed themselves in the skies of daybreak and sunset. There came a restlessness and fearfulness among the wild things of the earth. They were seen prowling in places where they had never ventured before, drawing near to the dwellings of man as if for refuge, and driven away with blows and curses. The radiance even of noonday became sad and sickly, though but little cloud was to be discerned in the firmament. In the midst of night strange lamentations, as if from bodily wanderers, broke the stillness. The pitch-black ark, its timbered roof glistening in the wan light, lay heavily on ground cracked in all directions in the windy heat of the day, for the earth was stark with drought, and the great door in its side gaped wide.

And the word of the Lord God came to Noah, bidding him go into the ark and take into it all the living creatures that were to be saved alive from destruction. So Noah and his three sons made a bridge of timber of a strength that would bear the tread of the mightiest beasts then on earth. This they laid between the door of the ark and firm ground; then each according to its kind, every living creature which they had in keeping and readiness for this day was brought into the ark, and there tethered or chambered in the places set apart for them. Two by two, and mate with mate they brought them in.

The greatest beasts and those whose habit it was to rove by night and sleep by day were given their places in the lowermost storey of the ark, beneath its undermost deck. The shy and delicate were cribbed where the light could shine in on them from the window. To each was its own particular place set apart in the pens and chambers within the hive-like confines of the ark. So too with the winged things, and with the scaled. Behemoth was there, and there, too, the mouse. All things that lived and moved, and had their being on the earth around them, found refuge there. They entered in from the sunlit plain into the gloom of the great ship. They entered into it, as though into a haven, from ills of which they had some faint forewarning, and none languished or pined or fell away in spirit or refused to eat.

Moreover, in the bins and chests and baskets which had been made ready and stood all in order and in place where they would be needed, Noah and his sons had laid up an abundant store of grain and hay and fodder and seed. Of all herbs and plants too, that would retain their virtue and nourishment for many days to come. These were for the food and sustenance of the beasts and the birds and the creeping things.

They hastened now to finish their preparations, for warnings abounded that the dreadful hour drew near. In the midst of his labours one or other of them would hastily lift his eyes to scan the heavens, so grievous were the signs which now showed themselves there and on the earth beneath. And they redoubled their efforts for fear that anything should be left unready and undone.

As for the least of the little things that haunt the air and solitudes and crevices of the earth, they seemed of their own wisdom to have already set up their habitations in the ark. The queen bee and her myriad workers made their cluster there; and the wise ant her nest. Butterflies on their painted wings floated out of the sunbeams into the dusk within, and of the lesser birds some had even built their nests on the ledge that ran beneath the long narrow window made for the coming-in of the light under the ark's dark roof.

When all the animals and birds, the reptiles and creeping things were safely within the ark, then Noah gathered his family together, his wife, his three sons, Shem, Ham and Japheth, and their wives, and their children. The last wild yellow light of evening dyed the heavens when in awe and dread they went up into the ark. And to each was given a sleeping-place in the great inner chamber wherein they were to spend the days that were to come. And when they had one and all crossed over into the ark, the bridge of timber was flung to earth, and the massive door turned upon its staples and was shut.

A cold trumpeting wind had begun to blow, lifting into the air dense clouds of sand and dust. It increased hour by hour, until nothing could be heard from within the ark but the sound of it streaming across the high rounded roof and wailing in every nook and cranny. Lightnings wild and luminous flared in the skies, but at first without sound of thunder. And when the tempest of wind began to lull, there fell the first few drops of rain.

The rain increased in volume until it seemed to those safe in the shelter of the ark as if sky and earth had mingled together in a dreadful confusion. The wells and fountains of the deep were broken, the rock-bound water-courses foundered, and the windows of heaven were opened. The deluge descended upon the ridged roof of the ark in a steady sullen roar and surged against its sides. Hour followed hour and even the huge wooden walls of the great ship trembled beneath the cataracts of the rain. And soon from its long window nought was visible but a world lost in water and lit by lightnings. And at length the ark that till then had lain upon the earth as if no force could so much as stir its enormous keel, was lifted as if by a gentle but mighty hand, swayed, came to rest again, heaved upward, and at length floated upon the waters.

When Noah and his three sons had gone their way to and fro in every part of the great ship, carrying with them the lamps they had moulded out of clay and filled with oil and a wick, and examined it in every part and returned together and reported nothing amiss, they gave thanks to God for their salvation.

And darkness, furious, awful and distraught, drew over the flooded plain, whose encircling mountains were already veiled from view with the wrack and cloud of tempest. Shrill outcries and lamentations were borne faintly in on the blast of the winds, but at last died down and were heard no more, unless from very far away. And the children were laid to rest in the sleeping-places prepared for them.

But during that first night little sleep visited those who watched over them. There were stirrings and sighings and snortings as the beasts they had in charge snuffed the frag-

rance of the waters of the deluge and were disquieted by the
din and tumult. They shared a narrow solitude in that chaos
of water.

But as the days went by there came peace and tranquillity
within the ark, and at length the humans within it grew so
accustomed to the endless gushings of the rain upon roof
and walls, that they were no longer troubled or dismayed,
and the sound of it at last became almost unheeded.

Buoyant yet stable upon the face of the deluge, the ark
floated beneath the louring skies whithersoever wind and
water led, in a mist so dense no eye could discern where
cloud and water met. But those within its walls, and in the
safety of God, went about their daily tasks, portioning out
the grain and fodder they had stored up within it, and
tending the living things they had in their charge, in trust

and confidence that they would be delivered at last from the danger and desolation that beset them.

For forty days and forty nights the rains continued without pause or abatement, and so obscure were the skies, that the light of dawn was hardly to be discerned when it began, or the oncoming of darkness when nightfall descended upon the deep.

The hours of sleep were divided into watches, Noah's three sons taking each his turn, so that nothing should go amiss and remain undiscovered, for each made his rounds according to the time set for him, passing from one storey to another and ensuring that all was secure.

There came a day at last when the roar of the deluge began to diminish, and the wind to fall to calm. And the fountains of the deep were sealed, and the rain from heaven was restrained.

There was now quiet on high above the earth. But a deep gloom still prevailed within the ark because of the prodigious canopy of cloud that obscured the whole firmament. All sounds, except the stir and callings within the wooden walls of the ark, were now hushed. And though there was movement in the clouds above, amid a vast sea of light where their fleeces were smitten to silver by the sun, nothing of this could be perceived from the window of the ark. Until one morning in his watch before dawn Shem stood peering out alone across the tumultuous waste of waters. And lo, as he looked he descried afar off a faint yet dazzling strip of silver between earth and heaven on the margin of the deep. His heart leapt within him, for he knew that it was the radiance of the rising of the sun, and that he was looking towards the quarter of the horizon which is the east.

He ran at once with these glad tidings to Noah, and they

awakened Ham and Japheth and their mother and their wives and their children, and all rose up hastily and gathered together at the window and gazed out, their minds filled with a joy beyond all words, their eyes exulting in this first gleam of the veiled radiance of the clouded sun. There they knelt and prayed together, and gave thanks to the Lord God.

Hour by hour the light increased, and the bitter surges of the deluge sank to rest, until at last even the blue of heaven began to show. But all around the ark, as far as sight could reach, there stretched a sea of water, green and placid, though blackened here and there with ghastly wreckage. It sparkled in the sunbeams, so that human eyes unaccustomed to the glare were almost blinded as they watched. And ever and again the mighty mastless vessel heaved on the slow swell that moved across the deep, rose, and dipped again. The ocean of waters seemed to be lulling itself to sleep with long-drawn sighs.

Moreover, not only the light but the heat of the sun now began to steal its way into the confines of the ark. Through a crevice of the window the bees found out an egress and sipped the dew on the roof and the nectar of the few blossoming weeds that had found harbourage there. The birds preened their wings and broke into merry wild-hearted song, whose voices for many days had been still and mute. Their sweet-billed notes rang shrill in the stealing sunshine.

From storey to storey, pen to pen, and chamber to chamber of the ark, the beasts called the joyous news from one to the other, for happy life began to stir again within them; and the desire for freedom, for the woods and pastures, valley and mountain, to move in their blood.

But though to all seeming the rains were now over and gone, no sign of land was anywhere detectable above the waters, nor even, as far as could be discerned, through the mists that veiled the horizon, did any mountain peak as yet uprear its crags. Yet morning, noon and evening the waters which had prevailed upon the earth continued to abate.

And the Lord God remembered Noah, and those who were with him in the ark. He caused a warm and gentle wind to pass over the earth, enveloping the waters. They diminished continually until at length and in all surety there showed afar off a mountain-crest jutting out above the flood into the sapphire skies, as if fashioned of crystal and alabaster.

Then Noah, considering within himself, chose from among the birds in his keeping a raven, and opening the window of the ark, he loosed it out of his hand. With one clap of its wild wings it darted out into freedom, and in the twinkling of an eye both the bird and its image reflected on the glass of the waters had fled away and vanished out of sight, never to return. For it found food in such abundance on which to glut itself in the wreckage of the flood, that it came back to the ark no more.

Noah waited for seven days, then took a dove and released her from the window of the ark. But the dove, that is a tender bird, found no rest for the sole of her foot where she could be content, for still the waters of the deluge covered the face of the earth, and she returned to the ark and fluttered at the window. So Noah put out his hand and drew the dove back into the safety of the ark.

He waited yet another seven days, then set her free again, and behold, as they stood watching at even-fall, she came again to the window of the ark, her snowy breast and plumage dyed with the rose of sunset, her round eyes gleaming. There she alighted; but now she brought with her in her bill a tender young olive leaf that she had plucked off from its stem, and Noah knew that the waters were indeed abated and assuaged from the earth.

And when he sent her forth again, she too returned to him no more.

The ark rested at last in the hollow between the peaks of Ararat, the high mountains of Armenia, and Noah and his sons removed its timber roof from off it, and they looked down upon dry ground. And the Lord God bade Noah come forth from out of the ark, himself and his wife, his sons and their wives and children.

"Bring out with thee", said the Lord God, "every living thing that is with thee in the ark, beast and bird and creeping thing, that they may be fruitful upon the earth and multiply."

Then the sons of Noah took of the timber which they had stripped from the ark and made a bridge of wood, and they thrust open the great door and let down their wooden bridge. And Noah with all his household went forth out of the ark under the blue of heaven in the burning sunshine upon the earth again, now wondrously flourishing in the sweet airs of the morning. They lifted their pale faces and breathed deep, and they walked together upon the solid earth; and the cries of the children resounded with delight, echoing against the weed-bearded sides of their great weather-worn ship.

That morning was spent in setting free the host of living things, all in order and each according to its kind, which had shared with them the safety of the ark and which they had fed and tended throughout the days of the flood.

Rejoiced they were to snuff the sweet free air of morning, and a mellay of cries and challengings rose from their throats, as they leapt and fawned and gambolled, shaking their shaggy coats, preening and sleeking themselves and marvelling in the sunlight. It was as if for the time being the peace of Eden had come upon the earth again, for during the many days of their dwelling within the ark they had become at peace one with another and with those who watched over them, and the enmity which the wickedness and cruelty of man had brought upon the earth had lost its sharpness, and for a while fears and doubts of him were stilled.

Then Noah built an altar to the Lord God and made sacrifice to him. And the Lord God blessed Noah and his sons and gave them the earth for their possession, and the lordship over all living things upon it for their use and care. He bade Noah and his sons go out into the world with their wives and children and seek each his own dwelling, so that their children's children should increase upon the earth and live at peace one with another, praising him who had given them life.

And as Noah and his household worshipped before the Lord, a faint mist, high in the noonday firmament, shaped itself across the blue as if it were a veil between heaven and earth, and the rays of the sun smote on the mist, and a great bow of broken light, burning with all the radiant colours that show upon the earth and in the waters and that are reflected in every living thing, flower and insect, beast and plumed bird, spanned the peaks of Ararat, where Noah and his household were gathered together with their possessions about the empty ark. It arched the green world over; and the light of day smote fair upon their upturned faces.

And the Lord God said to Noah: "Behold, I have set my bow in the clouds, and it shall be a token of an everlasting covenant between me and thee and all that come after thee, that never more shall there be a flood to destroy the earth where the life that I have created hath its dwelling. But after the rain shall shine the sun, and this bow that I have set in heaven shall be a sign of the covenant between the Lord God and his living creatures upon the earth, for evermore."

JOSEPH

His Dream

After the death of his father Isaac, Jacob, with his whole household, his sons, his servants, his flocks and herds and sheep-dogs, came to sojourn in the green and wooded vale of Hebron which is in Canaan. Here they pitched their tents, and led their flocks afield, for Hebron lies in a country rich in pastures and in clear well-springs of water.

Now of all his eleven sons Jacob loved Joseph the best. Until Benjamin was born, he was the youngest of them all, and he was too the only son of his beautiful mother Rachel, who was very dear to Jacob. Not only for this reason but for the child's own sake also, Joseph was Jacob's best-beloved; and, with no thought of any ill that might come of it, he favoured him in all things, delighted to talk to him, and he gave him many presents.

He made him also a loose tunic coat of many colours, sewn together in delicate needlework in a bright pattern, and with sleeves to the wrists. And Joseph, being in age still little more than a child, delighted in his bright-coloured coat. But when his brothers saw it, they envied and hated him. For in this his father had yet again shown his great love for Joseph and had favoured him above themselves, and they could not speak a friendly or peaceable word to him.

As Joseph grew older, and in all that he was and did showed himself more and more unlike themselves, jealousy gnawed in their hearts like the fretting of a canker-worm. Above everything, they scorned, and even began to fear him, because of his dreams. They too, as they lay with their flocks, wrapped in their goat-skin cloaks beneath the dews and burning stars of the night, had their dreams; but these either vanished on waking or were broken and senseless. But the dreams that came to Joseph in his sleep were not only of a strange reality, but seemed to carry with them a hidden meaning. They were like the crystal shimmering pictures of the air, called *mirage*, seen by wanderers in the desert, the reflections of things afar off—but far off in time not in space.

One late summer evening when he chanced to be with them in the fields, and sat a little apart from them, lost to all around him in the light of the moon—a moon so dazzling clear that even the colours of his coat were faintly distinguishable—they asked him sourly what ailed him.

"He sits out there", said one of them, "mumbling his thoughts like an old sheep too sick to graze." Joseph answered that he had been haunted all day by the memory of a dream. He was but a boy and he told his dream out to them, thinking no evil.

"I dreamed", he said, "it was the time of harvest, and we were reaping together in the fields. It was sunrise, and the corn being cut, we were tying it up into sheaves. Even now I seem to feel the roughness of the binder in my hand, though the place we were in was none I have ever seen in waking. I tied up my sheaf and laid it down, as you did your sheaves. And in my dream the sheaf that I had bound rose up as if of its own motion from the stubble and stood up there in the burning sunshine, and your own sheaves, that lay scattered around it, rose up also. And as I looked, they bowed themselves and made obeisance to my sheaf that was in the midst of them. Now what can be the meaning of such a dream, and why does it stay so continually in my mind?"

His brothers tried in vain to hide their anger.

"Meaning, forsooth!" they said. "Who art thou that we should bow ourselves down before thee, and that thou shouldst have dominion over us? The place for thee is with the women and sucklings in the tents." And they hated him the more.

Joseph was silent and made no answer, but the dream in its strangeness and beauty stayed on in his mind. He knew it must surely have a meaning, if only he could discover it; and when he dreamed again, he told his dream not only to his brothers, but to his father.

"I dreamed," he said, and his face was lit up at memory of it, "and, behold, in my dream it was the dead of night, yet the sun was in the heavens and the moon also. They shone there together, and I could see the stars. There was no wind, and all was still; and I counted the brightest stars, and they were eleven. And as I looked and wondered, it seemed that not only these eleven stars, but the sun and the moon stooped and bowed in their places in heaven before me and made obeisance. Then I awoke."

His brothers listened with louring faces, glancing covertly one at another, but Jacob his father rebuked him.

"Cast such crazy fancies out of thy mind," he said. "And God forbid that it should be even so much as in thy dreams that I and thy mother and thy brethren should come to bow ourselves down before thee and be humbled before thee!" None the less, the dream disquieted him, and there came a day when he remembered it again.

It chanced one evening after this, and when Joseph had passed his seventeenth birthday, that his father called him into his tent. He bade him set out on the morrow and go in search of his brothers, who had led their sheep to new pastures beyond the vale of Hebron, and not far distant from a town called Shechem.

"Go thy way early and seek them out," he said, "for they are among strangers and enemies. Ask them how they fare, and see thyself if it be well with them and with the flocks; and when you have rested, bring me word of them again. And may the Lord watch over you!"

Proud and happy in the trust his father put in him, Joseph rose up at daybreak next morning, kissed him, bade him good-bye, and set out at once. The day was calm and fair. It was springtime, the air was sweet with birds, and on the wayside and in the hollows of the hills hosts of wild flowers shone in their colours in the sun, crocus and anemone and narcissus. And as he went on his way, no omen chilled his heart of what was in store for him, and no foreboding that every step he took was towards a strange country from which in this life he would return home again no more.

He came at length to Shechem, an old walled and beautiful city of Samaria that with its gardens lay in a valley between two mountains, and rang with the music of more than a score of water-springs. But his brothers were no longer there, and loth to return to his father without news of them, he pressed on into country unknown to him, and lost his way.

A stranger met him as he was wandering at random in the wild. He saw how young he was, and that in spite of being anxious and footsore he still held on his way, so he hailed him and inquired whom he was seeking.

"It is my brothers," he said. "They are shepherds, but have gone on from Shechem where I looked to find them, and now I have lost my way. Tell me, I pray thee, what place is this and where it is likely they have gone?"

It chanced that this man had not only seen the shepherds but had overheard them in talk one with another, and he told Joseph they were now in all likelihood with their flocks near Dothan.

"It lies", he said, "on a hillside above its vineyards where there is a plentiful well of water." And he told him how he would find it. He repeated what he had said, "Follow on as I have told thee, and thou canst not miss the way."

He turned and watched until Joseph was out of sight. And Joseph hastened on eagerly, all weariness forgotten. Now on the northern side of Dothan there were hills, their slopes shagged with grey-green groves of olives, but on the side towards the south, it was flat country, so that his brothers, who were sitting there with their flocks and staring idly out across the grassy plain, spied out Joseph while he was still afar off. And they muttered morosely one to another: "Behold, the dreamer cometh!"

As they watched him making his way towards them in a coat of many colours, the hatred that had long smouldered in their hearts broke into flame, and some of them began devising together to murder him.

"He is alone and at our mercy," they said. "And here there is none to heed his cries or tell the tale. Let us kill him, then, and hide his body where it will never be found. Then we can go back with a tale that a wild beast must have attacked and devoured him. And who shall deny it?"

But Reuben, the eldest, overheard them muttering together. "No, no; shed no blood," he said. "If you must be rid of him, take him alive and fling him into that pit yonder. But use no violence, or let any harm come to him."

This he said because he himself intended, when the opportunity came, to set Joseph free, and to bring him back in safety again to his father. The rest of them argued and wrangled, some on this side and some on that, but at length they agreed together not to kill him. When Reuben was sure of it, and that no harm would come to Joseph until he could come back and take him into a place of safety, he left them and went away alone.

Joseph drew near, rejoiced to be at the end of his long journey and to see his brethren sitting in peace together with their flocks. But before he could so much as give them greeting or tell them why he had come, they seized him, stifled his cries, stripped off his coat of many colours, and bound him hand and foot. They carried him off to a deep dried-up pit or water-cistern. Into this pit they flung him down, and having dragged back the heavy stone again that had lain over the mouth of the pit, they left him there, returned to their camping-place, and sat down to eat.

While they were eating together, some jesting and others silent and uneasy, they heard in the distance shouts and voices borne on the windless air over the flat country. They lifted up their eyes and saw afar off a company of Ishmaelites, merchantmen, with their camels. These fierce swarthy tribesmen were journeying from Gilead which lay beyond the Jordan, a region famed for its balsam and groves of tree laurel, musical with the murmur of wood-doves and songs of birds. They were following the track of the great caravans that would bring them to the sand-dunes on the coast of the Great Sea, and then, on, and at length into Egypt. Their camels, neckleted with chains of metal, their links shaped like the crescent moon, were laden with sweet-smelling spiceries and fragrant gums which they had brought with them to barter or sell to the Egyptian embalmers and physicians.

When Judah, who had sat silent and aloof, saw these men with camels, he said to his brethren: "See now, here is a way out. If we leave the lad in the pit, he will perish of thirst and we shall be no less guilty of his death than if we had killed him with our own hands. Let us hail these accursed Ishmaelites, and sell him for what he will fetch. That way we shall see some profit in what we do, and we shall be for ever rid of him and his dreams. But not death, I say—for is he not our brother, the son of our father, and of our own flesh and blood?"

To this, though sullenly, they agreed. It was near sunset when, dragging away the heavy well-stone again, his brothers drew Joseph up out of the pit and freed him from the thongs with which they had bound him. He stood half-naked and trembling, faint with the heat of the pit. The sun smote blindingly on his eyes after the pitchy darkness in which he had lain—beaten and bruised and unable to stir hand or foot. He watched, while his brothers bargained with the crafty dark-browed Ishmaelites. They agreed at last to sell him to them for twenty pieces of silver, and divided the money between them. This done, the Ishmaelites knotted the cord that still shackled Joseph's wrists to the saddle of one of their camels, and continued on their way.

When Reuben came back at nightfall to the pit, called, and found it empty, he was smitten with remorse. He rent his clothes—as was the custom with these wandering tribesmen when to their anguish any great grief or disaster befell them—and he returned in despair to the camping-place. There he found his brethren and their flocks, hedged about with branches of thorn as a protection against wild animals.

"The lad is gone," he said, "and I, whither now shall *I* go?" But some of them pretended to be asleep, and none made answer.

Next day they killed a kid and dabbled Joseph's coat in its blood, then turned homewards with their flocks, and came at length to their own place and to their father's tent, and, with the pretence of grief on their faces, stood before him. His first thought was for Joseph, but he looked in vain for him.

Jacob questioned them anxiously. And when he told them how Joseph had been sent out to seek them in the valley of Shechem, they stared one at another, as though in horror and dismay. Then one of them named Simeon took out the torn and blood-bedabbled coat and spread it out before him.

"We knew nothing of what thou sayest until now," he said. "But on our way back from Dothan where we lay, we passed by a thicket of thorn trees in a wild and solitary place, and we found this. It is so bedraggled and drenched with blood that we cannot be sure if it be the coat you gave Joseph. See now, is this thy son's coat, or no?"

Jacob looked and trembled and turned away. "It is my son's coat," he said. "My son, Joseph! An evil beast hath devoured him; Joseph is without doubt rent in pieces. I shall never see his face again!"

He bowed himself in his grief and wept. He rent his clothes, and put on sackcloth like one who goes in mourning for the dead, and withdrew himself from them all, and remained in solitude for many days. His daughters and his sons, grown sick of their own treachery, came to him in hope to comfort him, but he refused to be comforted.

"Beyond the grave," he said, "but not until then, we two shall meet again. And my son Joseph will see how I have mourned for him." And he continued to grieve for Joseph, so great was the love he bore him. Only in Benjamin, who was his youngest son, did Jacob find solace as time went by. He loved and treasured him not only for his own sake but because, now that Joseph was gone, he was the only child left of his mother Rachel, for she had died when he was born.

In Prison

After many days' journey, in scorching sun by day and starry cold by night, the Ishmaelitish merchantmen, with their camels and spices and other merchandise, came down into Egypt. There all that Joseph saw was new and strange to him. They made their way into the chief city of Egypt and pushed on through the babel of its thronged and narrow streets into the marketplace. Here they unladed their camels. On the morrow they took Joseph into the slave-market, where captives from all countries that bordered the land of Egypt were bought and sold. And Joseph himself was bought by an Egyptian whose name was Potiphar, a man of wealth and one of the king's high officers.

At first sight of his keen open face, though it was now haggard with pain and sleeplessness, Potiphar judged well of Joseph. Unlike most of his slaves, Joseph was not sent to labour in the fields and vineyards under a taskmaster, but was taken into Potiphar's house and became his personal servant.

And the Lord was with Joseph; he kept him in all perils. Whatever Joseph did, he did well. He prospered in the house of his master, the Egyptian. And seeing that in all things he was upright and faithful, Potiphar as the years went by gave Joseph more and more authority in his household, and at last made him steward or overseer over his servants and his slaves, not only those who were within the house, but also over his gardeners and the tenders of his orchards and vineyards. So entire was his trust in Joseph that he had no cares or anxieties apart from his office under Pharaoh the king, and knew nothing of what passed in his household except only what he himself had to eat and drink. In all that Joseph did, he was answerable to Potiphar alone.

Yet in age Joseph was still but a young man. He was of a natural courtesy, and he had an open and beautiful countenance. And Potiphar's wife, who had often cast her eyes on him as he went about his business in the house, began to lie in wait for him and to pine for his company. She was a woman false and vain, and by all the deceits she knew she strove to beguile him, and at last spoke openly of her love. But he hated her, mind and body, and refused to listen.

"I entreat thee", he said, "say no more. My lord has shown me many kindnesses. He has made me chief of all his servants, and so complete is his trust in me that when at evening he returns home, he does not even question me on what has passed in the house during his absence. Everything and everyone in it has been given into my charge except only thee thyself; for thou art his wife. How vile a thing would it be, then, if I were to deceive him and sin against God."

Day followed day, and still the Egyptian's wife continued to pester him, until there came a morning when, they being alone together, lovesick and shameless, she once more besought him. He turned from her with loathing, and fled out of the house. And she knew at last that her deceits were in vain. Her love, never else than false, corrupted instantly into bitter hatred. And having proof that Joseph had been in her company, she set about to revenge herself against him.

She summoned the other chief servants of the household

and lied to them. "See now," she said, "this vile Hebrew whom my lord bought from the slave-traders and set up over you all! Why, he makes mock and insult even of me, the wife of his master. There is nothing safe from him."

That night when her husband was with her she lyingly accused Joseph, and this she did so guilefully, weeping, and as though in shame of having to confess what would anger and trouble him, that Potiphar believed her every word. He was beside himself with rage. He summoned his slaves and bade that Joseph should be bound and instantly cast into prison—the prison where offenders against King Pharaoh himself were kept in captivity. And Potiphar thought of him no more.

There Joseph lay, in a foul dungeon, and was set to such pitiless labour that when night came and the day was done, he was thankful to fling himself down in the darkness and forget his miseries in sleep. Yet in spite of all the hardships that he shared with the rest of the prisoners—driven and beaten and half-starved—he never gave up hope or lost courage. And the Lord was with Joseph in the prison. As time went on, his mere presence there became a solace to the wretchedness of those who languished with him, and the guards or warders spoke well of him, eased his labour and freed him of his fetters.

It thus came about that the governor of the prison having heard nothing but good of Joseph, began himself to show him favour. He discovered that this young Hebrew was not only a man whom he could trust in word and in deed, but that he was of a rare sagacity of mind, wise in counsel, swift in decision, and fearless in acting as he deemed right. At length he set Joseph next in authority under himself, and gave not only his chief captives into his charge but even the control of the prison.

Years passed by, and though Joseph was now no longer wretched in body, and had many things to busy his mind, the freedom he longed for seemed as far away as Canaan itself. Yet he did not repine; nor did he ever despair of his release at last. Whatever the days or the years might bring, he trusted in the Lord, and in that trust his mind was at peace.

Now there came a day when the chief butler and the chief baker of Pharaoh the King of Egypt—the one his cupbearer or high chamberlain and the other his steward—offended against their lord, the king. So hot was his wrath against them that he not only banished them from his presence, but commanded that they should be given into the charge of the governor of the prison, who was captain of the guard, until he himself had considered what punishment they merited.

These two, the chief butler and the chief baker, were men of high standing in the court of Pharaoh. Wherefore the governor of the prison bade Joseph himself attend on them, instructing him to show them the courtesies due to their rank and office, but none the less to be vigilant that they did not escape. Morning and evening Joseph waited upon them, and they found such solace in his company, and came so much to trust in his discretion that they would talk freely with him and confide in him their hopes and fears.

The days of their confinement in the prison had continued for many months when on one and the same night these two, the chief butler and the chief baker, dreamed each of them a dream, then awoke and dreamed no more. Even when daylight was come they could not rid their minds of what had troubled their sleep. And as they sat together in the room that had been set apart for them in the prison-house, they told one another their dreams. They were deeply troubled and perplexed, for their dreams were of a kind that seem to be haunted with a hidden meaning, yet neither of them could discover it or expound it the one to the other.

So it was that when Joseph came in to them in the morning, and greeted them, their voices were low and spiritless, and their faces dejected as if they had some burden on their minds. And though there were few in the prison under him who were never wretched and in despair, he did his utmost to enhearten all he could, not only because this was natural to him, but because he himself was in not much better case than they.

At last, looking upon these two as friend to friend, he questioned them. "Why", he said, "are your faces downcast, and why do you look so sadly this morning?"

The chief butler answered: "This night that is gone we have each of us dreamed a dream. Dreams closely resembling one another that have haunted our minds ever since, yet such we can neither understand nor forget. Were we free men, we could consult some diviner of dreams who would declare them to us and make them clear. But in this prison-house where shall we find anyone who has the least knowledge of the matter?"

"The divination of dreams", said Joseph, "is with God. I too have been a dreamer. Tell me your dreams, I might help you. It grieves me to see you so sad."

Then first the chief butler told Joseph his dream. It was in this wise. "I dreamed", he said, "I saw a vine, greener in its freshness to the sight than any vine my waking eyes have ever beheld. This vine had three branches, and little by little yet all in an instant and even as I watched, they broke into buds which themselves unfolded into blossom, and these having dropped their petals became clusters of green grapes that ripened and swelled before my very eyes. All in a moment the vine that had been winter-bare was heavy with fruit. And behold, the cup of the king, of King Pharaoh, was in my hand, though till then I knew it not. And I plucked a cluster of the grapes and pressed its juices into the cup, and it was wine; and I hastened in from the vineyard into the palace and gave the cup into Pharaoh's hand. Then I awoke, and could sleep no more."

Joseph listened. So intent was he on the words as they were spoken that he himself seemed to be lost in dream; and when the chief butler had fallen silent, and sat eagerly watching his face as he stood before them, he made answer like one deep in reverie.

"This", he said, "is the meaning and interpretation of thy dream. The vine thou sawest was the vine of Time, and the three branches upon it were three days which in life as we live it may come and go like shadows upon water, but which in thy dream budded, flowered, and bore clusters of ripe refreshing grapes all in a moment, and so—to Pharaoh the King. Be no more sad or downcast, but take comfort, for in three days thy troubles shall be over. Pharaoh will remember thee, and will show thee grace and restore thee into his favour, and thou shalt be his cupbearer and minister to him as of old. And oh!" he added, "when it is well with thee, I beseech thee of thy kindness remember me, and make mention of me to Pharaoh, and, if it may be, bring me out of this prison. Canaan is my country; I was sold into slavery when I was but a boy, and snatched away by force from the tents and pastures where I lived as a child, and from a father who loved me. And I have done nothing here that they should have cast me into a dungeon."

The chief butler, in the fullness of his heart, gladly promised Joseph all that he asked of him.

Meanwhile the chief baker had sat intently listening to all that had passed, his eyes in his narrow, hawk-like face fixed upon Joseph. And when he knew that there was nothing but good and fair in the chief butler's dreams, he at once related his own.

"This was my dream," he said. "I was walking—and no one by—in the open under the heavens, and there were three baskets upon my head, one on the top of the other. And I knew—though how I cannot tell—that in the uppermost of the three baskets were fine wheaten loaves of my own making for the king's table, and for the lords of his household. And this was a strange thing, for I am, you must know, by nature exceedingly careful of what is in my charge, and though the loaves were for the table of my lord the uppermost basket was uncovered. Now as I walked, the skies overhead became laden, overcast and dark. Wherefore I went on in haste to do my office, but the birds of the air, spying out these dainties, swooped down in a ravenous fluttering cloud over my head and I was powerless to scare them away. As I say, they came down upon me in a host, scrabbling upon the basket, and devoured everything that was in it. Now tell me, seeing that all is well, why were the heavens above me dark, and why was my topmost basket uncovered?"

On hearing this, Joseph turned away his head in distress and made no answer. The face of the chief baker wanned, but he pressed Joseph to speak; and Joseph was at last persuaded.

"May it be forgiven me," he said, "but this, alas! is the meaning of thy dream. As with the vine and its three branches, so the three baskets on thy head were a symbol of three days. In three days from this, Pharaoh the King will hale thee too out of this prison-house. But not for good. He has discovered some evil, and in his wrath he will hang thee on a tree, and the birds of the air shall eat thy flesh from off thy bones."

All came about as Joseph had foretold. On the third day after, Pharaoh made a feast to all his household, for it was his birthday; and his high officers and the lords and governors of his provinces were bidden to the feast, and there were rejoicings throughout Egypt.

As was his custom, Pharaoh commemorated his birthday by recalling to mind those of his officers and servants who had offended against him. To some he granted amnesty and pardon, and forgave them. And among these was his chief butler. He was recalled into favour and, as in former times, waited upon his lord the king as his cupbearer when he sat at meat.

As for the chief baker, Pharaoh's anger was hard against him, for much was revealed that had been hidden. He too was set free from prison, but to be hanged upon a gibbet. And the birds of the air stripped his bones of their flesh, and another man was appointed in his stead. So all things came to pass as Joseph had divined and foretold. Yet did not the chief butler remember Joseph, but forgot him.

Seeing at length that no help was to come from him, Joseph cast out of memory the longing that had sprung up in his heart that day, like a gourd after rain, and for the two years that followed continued to go about his duties as he was accustomed to in the prison-house.

He Divines Pharaoh's Dream

But there came a day when Pharaoh the king himself dreamed a dream, and was profoundly troubled in spirit.

It seemed he stood beside a river, and there came up out of its waters seven kine or cows, which fed together at the river's brink. And as his eyes watched them in his dream, they were followed by another seven kine, different in shape and appearance, which, browsing nearer, suddenly fell upon and devoured the seven that he had first seen. And he awoke.

When at length the drowsiness of sleep stole over his senses, he dreamed again. He saw, as it were, flourishing upon one stalk or stem seven full ears of corn. But as he looked and wondered, there sprouted out on the same stem another seven, black and mildewed, which so utterly defaced and destroyed the full ears that nothing of them remained. Again he awoke, shaken and cold with dismay.

Sleep returned to him no more that night. He lay weary and restless, pondering on the two dreams, which unfolded themselves again and again before his waking eyes as vividly as in sleep. But however intently he considered them and compared them one with another, he could draw out of them no semblance of a meaning for the reality of day. Yet he was assured in his heart that these dreams were no mere idle shows of the night, but had been sent to warn him, and held a meaning as yet hidden from him.

Even when the fair beams of morning lit up his great chamber windows and the day had begun, his mind was no less disquieted and dark with foreboding. So he summoned his diviners and magicians—men who were wise in the interpretation of dreams and of omens. With heads shaven, and in their white mantles, they came into his presence, made obeisance, chaunted his praises, and stood awaiting his pleasure.

But when he had told them his dreams, they were one and all at a loss to expound them. And though they debated long together, and each of them did his utmost by every means of magic and sorcery that he knew to discover a meaning, there was none of his diviners that satisfied Pharaoh or in whom he could put his trust. He dismissed them from his presence with displeasure. And when the chief butler, who was waiting upon him, saw in what disquietude of mind the king was, and how even the most cunning of his soothsayers had been unable to interpret his dreams, there sprang up in his mind remembrance of the long heavy weeks that he had shared in captivity in the prison-house with the chief baker, now long dead, and how their cares had ended.

That evening, as Pharaoh sat at table, he asked leave to speak to the king. "Thy servant", he said, "hath this day been reminded of the past and of a promise that he made but that until now he has failed to keep; for which he is greatly to blame. Pharaoh may of his grace remember that some time ago he was offended with his servant, and also with his servant who was at that time the chief baker in Pharaoh's palace. And we were both of us put under ward of the governor of the prison, both myself and the chief baker. One night—after many weary days of banishment from Pharaoh's presence—we dreamed a dream, both I myself and he, and were greatly troubled. For our dreams seemed to have some meaning, though we knew not what it was. Next morning we told one another our dreams, which were much of a likeness one with the other, and we were sorely perplexed by them. And there came in, as was usual, a young man, a Hebrew, the servant of the governor of the prison, who waited upon us. We had spoken with him before, and thought well of him and of his understanding and courtesy. And each in turn we told him—the chief baker and myself—our dreams. And behold, even as he expounded them to us, so everything came to pass. My lord the king, of his mercy, restored me into his favour, and made me his cupbearer again, even as I am to this day. But the chief baker did not find favour in Pharaoh's eyes, and was hanged."

"What manner of man", said Pharaoh, "was this young Hebrew?"

"He was a young man of a rare wisdom and of a beautiful countenance. The governor of the prison-house thought well of him, and it grieves me that I have forgotten him so long."

Then Pharaoh sent messengers to the governor of the prison, and bade him (if this young Hebrew were still alive) deliver him up without delay, and bring him into the presence of the king. Whereupon the governor of the prison sent in haste for Joseph to do the king's bidding, and told him that Pharaoh himself had sent for him. They were by now friends together, servant and master, and he spoke kindly to him, and wished him well, and lent him suitable clothes in which to appear before the king. So Joseph shaved himself, put off his prison clothes, and changed his raiment, and was brought into the vast pillared council hall of the royal palace, and into the presence of Pharaoh himself.

Surrounded by his priests and diviners, his noblemen and
officers of state, some among them men of Syria and
Ethiopia and of Nubia, chosen from near and far for their
sagacity or valour or influence to serve him, Pharaoh was
seated upon a dais under a canopy. He was garbed in a
robe of fine linen adorned with gold and coloured enamel.
His chair of state was of gold. Two serpent heads of gold
couched on his temples. Beside him stood his fan-bearers.
When Joseph had been brought in, he made obeisance to

[83]

Pharaoh, bowing with his face to the ground before him, and stood whe : he was. But Pharaoh bade him draw near, and looking gravely upon him, spoke with him—these two together.

"I have dreamed a dream", he said, "which the spirit within me assures me has a meaning that is of moment—and a meaning moreover of which I should be made speedily aware. But there is none among my priests and diviners who can expound it to me. It has been told to Pharaoh that thou thyself art possessed of a natural under-standing of dreams, and a divination to pierce through their strange disguises to what they intend. Is that so?"

And Joseph answered the king: "The interpretation of dreams is with God, and only he of his wisdom can give the insight to divine this dream."

Pharaoh stooped forward a little where he sat. "So be it," he said. And he told Joseph his dream.

"I dreamed", he said, "I stood upon the bank of a great river in flood. And as I stood musing there, looking upon the turbid flowing waters, behold, there came up out of the river seven kine. They came up, I say, out of the river—sleek, well-nourished beasts, and comely. They browsed to-gether in the green sedges in the pastures of the marsh by the brink of the river. And as I looked, yet another seven kine came up from out of the river; but these were beasts lank and deformed, dreadful to look upon and ominous. In-deed I have never seen their like before in the whole land of Egypt. These also stood grazing awhile, and in so doing, drew near to the other seven. And it seemed in my dream—more swiftly even than I can recount it now—that of a sudden the lean lank cows fell upon and utterly devoured the seven that were sleek and comely. Yet could no mortal eye see any change in them. They were none the better for it, but remained as lean and lank as before. At this I awoke, troubled with an inward dread.

"When at length sleep returned to me, I dreamed again. But this dream is hard to tell, it was so swift in vanishing; and it appeared, as it were, all in the empty air. I saw upon one stalk seven ears of corn, full and fair and ripe for harvest, which yet in an instant were clean gone and vanished away, devoured by seven other ears, meagre and mildewed and smitten with the corruption of the burning blast of the east wind. Then I woke and could sleep no more.

"These then are the dreams that I have related to my magicians and diviners of secret things, and not one of them has yet been able to make clear their meaning to me, yet meaning my mind assures me they have."

He ceased speaking, and Joseph stood awhile silent before him, his face rapt and absent, his eyes fixed. Then he raised his head and looked on Pharaoh, and bowed himself before him and made answer:

"The two dreams", he said, "have one meaning, and in both of them God has revealed to Pharaoh what he is about to do. The river the king saw in his dream was the river of Egypt, which, like time, flows on continually, and year after year renews the harvest on which Pharaoh's whole realm and might depend. The seven cows that came up out of its waters were sign and symbol of seven years. So also with the dream of the harvest-field; the meaning of both dreams is the same. The first seven in each dream mean seven full and copious years—years of great plenty. So, too, with the seven lank and famished cows, and the seven ears of corn stricken and blasted with the east wind. These are seven years of famine. By Pharaoh's dreams God intended to reveal to him that a period of abundant harvests is coming to Egypt, and that the whole nation will rejoice in them. But after them will follow seven years of bad harvests, years of woe and dearth. So that not only will the seven good harvests be forgotten in Egypt, but the people will be in want and misery and will cry for bread. It was God's will that this should be revealed to Pharaoh in the dreams of sleep. Therefore Pharaoh dreamed twice, since two warnings are better than one. And what has been forewarned God himself will surely bring to pass."

Pharaoh pondered, his eyes fixed upon the face of Joseph, and he knew in his heart that the interpretation of his dreams which this young Hebrew had given him was the true meaning of them.

In this belief he questioned Joseph: "Verily I believe what thou sayest to be true. When, then, the seven evil years draw near, what hath thy God revealed to thee should Pharaoh do?"

Joseph considered within himself in silence a while. Then he answered Pharaoh that he should choose from among his counsellors a man wise and far-sighted, and to him should authority be given over all Egypt. Let this man, Joseph said also, appoint officers to serve under him, men of trust and repute, each in his own province throughout the land. During the seven years of plenty it should be their duty at the time of harvest to collect under the king's authority and each in his own province, a fifth of all the corn and wheat that had been grown in that province, and to store it in barns or granaries that should be built in the chief cities.

"By this means," said Joseph, "a vast store of grain will be gathered together and kept safe in the granaries, sealed under the seal of Pharaoh the King, and nothing of it during the first seven plentiful years shall be used or wasted. Then when the years of famine come, the doors of the granaries shall be opened, and the people will bring their money and buy food according to their need. Only thus can the disaster of famine be prevented, and the people shall realize the wisdom and foresight of the father of all, Pharaoh the King."

The wisdom of what Joseph had said was simple and clear, and yet showed a marvellous insight into affairs of state in one so young. His face, too, was animated and eager with his thoughts. He spoke like one who repeats what he hears as though it is prompted by a voice within him—one whose only thought is truth, having neither heed nor fear of aught else. Pharaoh fixed his regard on him with great care and intentness. He himself had a mind generous and able to perceive a wisdom that was yet beyond his own divining, as the moon gains her light from the sun.

At last he withdrew his eyes from Joseph and turned to the courtiers and counsellors that were about him. And they too marvelled.

Then said Pharaoh the King: "Where in all my realm shall we find one to excel, nay even to equal this man in wisdom and understanding, and in whom is the spirit of God?"

Then he turned again to Joseph: "I see", he said, "that the God of all is with thee, and there is none in all my realm can give me wiser counsel than thyself. To thee, then, do I entrust the doing and execution of all that thou hast advised. Full authority do I ordain to thee over the whole land of Egypt, to choose out able and trustworthy men to be officers over my provinces, to amass the corn during the years of plenty, to store the grain, and to obey thee in everything at pain of their lives as thou shalt direct. And all my people shall obey thee, according to my decree."

In token of this, Pharaoh took his signet ring from off his finger and put it upon Joseph's finger. And he arrayed

Joseph in a robe of fine linen such as was worn only by the chief lords of Egypt and by the king's counsellors. Over this he hung about Joseph's neck a chain of fine gold. And Pharaoh gave command that a chariot should be prepared for Joseph that in beauty and richness of workmanship should be but second to his own. Thus Pharaoh appointed Joseph lord over all the land of Egypt.

"I am the Pharaoh," he said, "and this is my decree: that not a man shall stir hand or foot in all Egypt without thy consent." Pharaoh, moreover, gave Joseph a name which he himself had chosen, *Zaphnath-paanear*, meaning thereby the saviour of the land, or the revealer of secrets.

From that day onwards, apart from Pharaoh himself, Joseph was first in Egypt in rank and power. He was thirty years of age when he was made Pharaoh's chief counsellor or vizier. When the king in his splendour, attended by his courtiers and high officers and with his guard of horsemen, rode out in state from city to city throughout the land of Egypt, the chariot of Joseph followed next after his own. And a herald or runner went on before his chariot to announce his coming. And the people in the streets and all who waited everywhere to watch and to see him, bowed the knee to Joseph as he passed by, hailing him with acclamations of " '*Abrek!* '*Abrek!* Lo, now pay heed. Behold the lord of all!"

By the grace of Pharaoh also, Joseph took to wife Asenath, the daughter of a prince of Egypt named Potipherah, who was priest of the Temple of the Sun in the city of Heliopolis or On.

As he had foretold, the harvests of the seven years that followed were marvellously rich and plenteous. In all things according to his command, the officers or stewards whom he had appointed to serve under him collected a fifth of all the crops in Egypt, and laid it up in many-chambered granaries. These—in cities where there was none already for the feeding of the king's army and his slaves—had been built for this purpose. In every city was a granary wherein was hoarded the grain that was not needed for food in the country surrounding it. The corn thus accumulated throughout Egypt was at last like the sand of the sea for abundance, so that no strict account could be taken of it, for the plenty of it passed all measuring.

In these years two sons were born to Joseph. The first he named Manasseh, a word that means, "Causing to forget", for, as he said to Asenath, the mother of his son, "God hath made me forget the travail that is gone." And his second son he called Ephraim, which means, "Fruitful", for God had made him to grow and to flourish and had blessed him in a strange land wherein first he had had nothing.

But the seven years of plenty came to an end, and they were followed by seven years of extreme dearth and famine. During these years the mighty river of Egypt which in its annual season flooded the country on either side of its banks, leaving behind it when its waters fell away a rich silt or sediment without which the arid sunbaked sands of Egypt would have borne no crops at all, had flowed further inland than in living memory it had ever flowed before. But in the next seven years its waters ran scant and shallow, so that only a narrow ribbon of land on either side of the dwindling river could be sown with seed. Nor was the famine in Egypt alone, but in all the countries surrounding it.

When the people of Egypt had consumed what corn they had themselves saved and laid aside from their good harvests, and were in great need, they appealed to Pharaoh for food. And Pharaoh made proclamation that any in want should come to Joseph, who, as his vizier, had power to ordain all things as seemed best to him.

Then Joseph gave orders to the stewards whom he had appointed in the cities of Egypt that the granaries and storehouses which were stuffed to their roofs with grain, their entries sealed with Pharaoh's seal, should now be opened up, and that corn should be sold to all that came to buy. And as from time to time he decreed, so was the price fixed.

When rumour spread far and wide that while there was famine in all the countries neighbouring on Egypt, there was plenty in Egypt itself, there came strangers and aliens from all parts into Egypt to buy corn. It had become the warehouse of the world. And Pharaoh's treasuries were filled to overflowing with the money that was paid to the stewards of the granaries, both by the Egyptians and by the strangers that came from afar with their caravans, their camels and their asses. There, none was poor and none hungry.

As in all the countries bordering on Egypt, so it was in the land of Canaan, and even in the well-watered and fruitful vale of Hebron, where in their tents dwelt Jacob and his sons. Their harvest had failed again and yet again. The earth was parched up in the heat of the sun. The pastures near and far lay bare and dry. Their flocks and herds were perishing for lack of grass and fodder, and there was an extreme dearth. So great was their need that their store of corn would soon be at an end, and they knew not where to turn for help.

There came a stranger one evening to their tents who reported that there was not only corn in Egypt, but corn in such plenty that it was for sale to all who came, and that he himself was about to set out thither. Those of the sons of

Jacob who heard him, listened eagerly, but said nothing.

The stranger was entertained with what little hospitality they had to offer. And when he had bidden them farewell and gone his way, Jacob turned to his sons and said: "Why do you stand looking darkly and doubtfully one at another? What folly is this? Has not the man told us that there is corn in Egypt, and that we can buy there all we need? Up, and take money with you then, saddle your asses and set out without delay. Make all the speed you can, both in going and returning, that we may live and not die."

They turned from him without another word and began to prepare for their journey. On the morrow the ten brothers set out from Hebron, following the track of the great caravans that go down from Gilead into Egypt, as had the Ishmaelitish merchantmen two and twenty years ago, when for twenty shekels of silver his brothers had sold Joseph into slavery and he had been led off at the coming on of night, never to return.

But Jacob would not let Benjamin go with his brethren, lest peradventure any harm should come to him.

His Brothers in Egypt

D ay by day the great caravan which Joseph's ten brothers had joined with their asses was swollen with strangers of sundry races and tongues and with their beasts of burden. And in the midst of this barbaric concourse they came at last to the chief city of Egypt, where Joseph was now vizier or viceroy, second only in power and lordship to Pharaoh himself.

When with their money they entered the granary to buy corn, the clerks who kept tally of the corn mistrusted them at sight. First, because they were Hebrews, and next, because on being questioned they could give only a confused account of themselves, being unable to make themselves understood in the Egyptian tongue. The clerks brought them to the steward who had control of the granary, and he himself, having interrogated them and doubting what they said in answer, sent them under guard to the great hall of the vizier.

They were brought therefore into the presence of Joseph himself, where he sat surrounded by his officers and by those in attendance upon him. There they waited before him until he was at liberty to hear for what reason they had been brought thither. He raised his eyes at length, and bidding the steward come forward, saw these ten strangers awaiting his pleasure.

At sight of them his heart leapt within him. He knew instantly who they were, and longed to make himself known to them. Only joy was in his heart to see them; but first, he determined to test them and to discover how time had used and changed them. So he sat motionless and made no sign of recognition. They drew near, and bowed themselves before him with their faces to the earth.

And, as if the long years that had gone by had never been, the dreams of his boyhood returned into his mind— the sheaves of corn in the fields of harvest, and the stars in the night sky. But his brothers gazed at him only with awe and misgiving; they were troubled, being strangers in a strange land, and ignorant of why they were regarded with suspicion and mistrust. And they knew him not, for the years had much changed him. He had been but a stripling in his first youth when they had last seen him, bruised and bound and almost naked in the hands of the Ishmaelites. Now he was come to his full manhood, being thirty and nine years old, and he had seen many sorrows and afflictions. Besides which, he sat before them, grave and austere, and raimented in his robes of office, Pharaoh's chain of gold about his neck, his signet ring upon his finger. They knew only that they were in the presence of one who had supreme authority, and that their safety and perhaps their very lives were in his hands.

With countenance unmoved he heard the reasons given by the steward of the granary for their having been brought before him, though all that was said was past their own understanding. Then he called for an interpreter and, through him, addressed them as if they were not only men of no account but under sharp suspicion. He spoke harshly to them.

"Whence come you?" he asked them.

"From the land of Canaan," they answered

"And why?"

"We are come hither to buy food," they said.

But he pretended not to believe them. "Nay," he said, "that, it may be, is a reason simple enough as you think to deceive me. But I give it no credence. What proof of it have you? It is not to buy food that you are come hither, but rumour having reached you that there is dearth in Egypt and that its people are in distress, you are here to spy out the defences of the land. You are enemies of my lord the king. Treason is your aim. You are spies."

They protested, assuring him that this was not so. "Indeed, my lord," they said, "we are no spies, but peaceable men, shepherds. Our grain was all but spent, and our flocks and herds were dwindling daily for lack of pasture. The famine is very grievous in Canaan. And having heard that there was corn in Egypt, we set out with money to buy. But the men of the granary refused to sell to us."

"They did well," said Joseph. "For I perceive by your very looks and demeanour that you are spies—Hebrew spies. To see the nakedness of the land you are come."

"But indeed no, my lord," they pleaded, "for were we spies, we should not be together and in one company. Indeed we are ten brethren of one household, sons of one father, and——"

But Joseph broke in upon them. His countenance had darkened, though they knew not why. " 'Ten,' you say; have you then no other brother? Has this father you speak of no other sons?"

"Yea, my lord," they said, "there is the youngest. But he is very dear to our father and remains with him in Canaan. And there was yet another, but he is no longer with us. Indeed, my lord, thy servants are honest men, and no spies."

But Joseph still professed not to believe them. "Whether

what you say be true or false," he said, "I cannot yet tell. But I will put you to the proof. For by the life of Pharaoh, you shall not escape me until I have assurance that you are the shepherds of Canaan you say you are, and nought else."

Without further word, he gave orders that they should be kept in strict charge until he should have time and occasion to examine them again. They were thrust into prison and lay there three days, being treated not as captives condemned to punishment, but as men under arrest and suspicion. On the third day they were brought before him again.

Joseph told them that he had considered the account they had given of themselves. "Your lives", he said, "are in my hands; and of a surety, if what you tell me prove false, you are in very great peril. But my trust is in God, in whom is truth and justice. You profess to be harmless shepherds of sheep, sons of one father dwelling in Canaan. Hearken, then! I will believe you so far as to keep only one of you as hostage for the rest, until you return again. Begone out of Egypt at once, take with you the corn you came to buy, and go in haste, for if what you have said be true, your father and your wives and children may be in sore straits for want of food. But bear in mind that you do this only on one condition—namely, that without delay you return again into Egypt and to this city, bringing with you the youngest of you, this brother of whom you have spoken. By this alone shall I be assured of your honesty, and by this alone shall you save the life of the one among you who remains in bondage in Egypt. Else he shall surely die."

In low voices they talked anxiously one with another as they stood before him, debating what he had said, and wholly unaware that he knew their language, for this day also he had addressed them only in the Egyptian tongue, and by means of an interpreter who was familiar with the Hebrew.

The long hours of doubt and dread they had spent in the prison-house had brought the past before their minds, and though they had spoken with caution lest they should be overheard, there had been strife between them. For even remorse itself makes enemies of those who have conspired together in evil and treachery. But they had now made their peace one with another. "Assuredly", they were saying, "this judgment has fallen upon us because we are guilty, though not of what this man now charges us with. It is because of our brother Joseph that all these misfortunes have overtaken us. We saw the anguish of his soul when he entreated us to take pity on him, and we refused to listen."

And Reuben could not refrain himself. He reminded them bitterly: "Did I not implore you to spare the child, and not to sin against him and against his father? But you mocked me down and played me false. And now at last has come the day of reckoning—our blood for his."

Listening to their talk, and seeing their trouble and distress, Joseph was grieved for them. He withdrew himself away from them a little to hide his tears; for there were many memories in his mind between that day and this.

When he returned to them again, he gave orders that Simeon should be the one kept back as hostage for the rest. This he did because Simeon was next among them in age to Reuben, the eldest, and Joseph had not known until now that Reuben had interceded with them and saved his life when they had intended to kill him. Then Simeon was bound before their eyes, and a guard of soldiers haled him away to the prison. The rest of them Joseph dismissed from his presence without further speech with them. But meanwhile he had secretly instructed his steward to ensure that after they had been provided with what corn they required, each one of these Hebrews' money should be hidden in the mouth of his sack. He bade his steward, too, supply them with every thing they might need on their journey back to Canaan. And this was done.

So the nine brothers, their asses laden with corn and all that they needed, set out, and at night came to an inn or camping-place and rested there. When one of them that evening opened his sack to get provender for his ass, he espied to his amazement a bag of money in it—a leathern bag tied up in the mouth of the sack. He ran at once to tell the others of what he had found.

"This bag of money", he said, "must have been hidden in my sack, for it was certainly not there when we saddled our asses this morning. Shekel for shekel it is the price I paid for my corn."

At this their hearts sank within them. They knew not what evil might follow from it, and they were afraid.

When they were come into Canaan and had reached their journey's end, they told their father all that had happened to them while they had been away. "Without reason being given," they said, "we were seized, and taken before the man who is lord under Pharaoh over the whole land of Egypt. In power and honour he is next to Pharaoh himself. He treated us harshly and accused us of being spies. We answered him suingly and assured him that this was not so, that we were honest and peaceable men—ten out of twelve brethren, the sons of one father, and that of the other two, one is no more, and the youngest with you in Canaan. Yet he still refused to believe us. And we were taken away, and for three days lay in a dungeon, knowing not what evil would come on us next."

"How then", said Jacob, "did you escape out of his hands?"

"Why," said they, "when we were brought before him again, he spoke to us less harshly and said that he had decided to put our word to the proof. 'By this,' he said, 'I shall know whether you be honest men or no. One of you shall remain here in strict charge, and the rest of you shall take the corn you need. And now be gone!' he said. 'But take heed to me—for if you do not speedily return, bringing with you this younger brother of whom you have spoken, then shall I know—as I believe—that you have lied to me. And the one of you I hold in charge shall surely die.' Then Simeon was taken, and we made all haste away."

When Jacob heard this, he bitterly reproached them.

"What evil have I done that you bereave me of my children? Joseph is not; Simeon is not; and now you would take Benjamin from me. All these things are against me and I can do nothing."

Reuben grieved for his father and drew near to comfort him. He promised that if Jacob would consent to entrust Benjamin into his charge, he himself would bring him back unharmed and in safety. "And if I keep not my word with thee," he said, "thou mayest kill the two sons I leave behind me. There is nothing dearer to me on earth." But Jacob turned away and made no answer.

And when presently, after unlading their asses, they found, one and all, that the money which they had paid for their corn had been hidden in their sacks, they stared in consternation one at another, and were sick with foreboding.

They told their father of this, imploring him to let them return at once into Egypt. But he refused to listen.

"Nothing you can say will persuade me to let your brother Benjamin go with you. Joseph is dead. He too was but a boy when he went out to seek you in Shechem and came back to me no more. Now Benjamin is the only son left to me of my old age. If I were to consent to his going and any harm were to befall him while he was with you, it would bring down my grey hairs with sorrow to the grave."

The famine increased. The skies were like brass, the earth baked hard as brick, and there came no sign or hope of any relief. They waited on from day to day until the corn they had brought from Egypt was running perilously short and would soon be consumed. Their flocks and herds grew lank and sickly; even their little children were ailing for want of milk and nourishment. And Jacob could refrain himself no longer.

"There is not a day to lose," he said to his sons. "You must go at once and bring us a little food. And I myself will remain here with Benjamin."

And Judah once again, and as tenderly as words could, assured his father that this was impossible. "The man who was lord over Egypt, did solemnly swear and protest to us: 'By the life of Pharaoh', he said, 'unless, when you return, your brother be with you, you shall not see my face again!' If we venture without him, then not one of us, as I believe, will ever come back alive."

Then said Jacob: "Why did you deal so ill with me as to even mention to this man that you had a younger brother?"

"But he questioned us closely again and again," said his sons. "He inquired where we came from, who were our kindred, if our father were still living, if we ourselves were his only sons or had he yet another. How could we else, then, but answer him according to the tenor of his questions; how could we have evaded them? How, too, could we have foreseen that he would snatch at our words and say: 'Return and bring your brother with you'?"

Then Judah pleaded yet once again with his father. "Give the boy into my care," he said. "And let us set out at once. The corn we bought is all but gone, our little ones will soon be crying for food. If we stay now, death stares us one and all in the face. I myself will be surety for him, and if I fail to bring him back to thee safe and sound, be mine the blame for ever. For except we had lingered, we should by now have already gone and come back again."

Then said Jacob: "What must be, must be. Make ready at once and go. But do not venture empty-handed. Take the best of the little we have left and carry it down to this man for a present; a little balsam and some honey and storax, spices, nuts and almonds—whatever we have that is sought after by the Egyptians; and let it be our choicest. Take not only double money with you, lest, as I suspect, in these last months the price of corn may have risen, but take also the money that was hidden in the mouths of your sacks. That, maybe, was only an oversight, but will be proof of your honesty. And Benjamin shall go with you. Delay no more. And may God Almighty be with you and ensure you mercy when you come again into the presence of this man, that Simeon may be restored to you, and that he keep not Benjamin. But if it be God's will that I am to be bereaved of him, then I am bereaved." He wept and withdrew himself out of their sight.

He Reveals Himself

His sons with all haste prepared for their journey. They loaded their asses with the presents their father had bidden them take with them— honey, spices, balm, almonds—the best they had in store. They took with them also double money— twice the amount they had taken on their first going down into Egypt, and the money also which had been concealed in their sacks.

When everything was ready, Benjamin came out to them from his father, and they set out together. He was young and fearless, and he had his mother's beauty. And he was eager beyond measure to see the great lord of whom he had heard his brothers speak, and the cities and temples and tombs, and all the famed marvels of the land of Egypt, and the splendour of Pharaoh.

In due time they presented themselves before the steward of the granary. He sent word to Joseph that these Hebrews were come again, and that they had brought with them a lad who they said was their youngest brother. When Joseph heard this, his heart welled over with joy and happiness. He summoned his steward, the overseer of his household, as he himself had been under Potiphar: "Take these men to my house", he said, "and see that everything is done to put them at their ease and comfort, for they are to dine with me at noon."

So his steward himself went to the granary as he was bidden. There he found the Hebrews still in custody. He led them away through the streets of the city, reeking with dust and heat, and loud and busy with traffic. On either side of the crowded alleys were the shops of the goldsmiths and the sandal-makers. There, too, the barbers, cook-shops and pastry-cooks, potters and beer-houses. A throng of wayfarers of a score of different races jostled them on every side. Benjamin gazed about him in astonishment—at the Egyptians themselves, painted and bewigged, with their folded cloaks and long walking-canes; at the women tattooed on chin and brow, their hair dyed blue, with their collars of beads and precious gems and their tinkling bracelets. The scene was past comparison beyond anything he had ever dreamed or imagined.

The steward brought them at last, where all was quiet, to a gateway of carved stone, in the shade of a dark green acacia tree. Through this they entered the courtyard of Joseph's house. It was paved with stone, and from it terraces went down, set with pools and conduits of water, serene and glittering in the sun under the deep blue of the Egyptian skies. Lilies, the flower of the lotus, lay in bloom snowy and golden amid their flat green leaves in the water. Ducks of bright plumage floated upon it. It was screened with green trellises of vines.

Beyond, they looked out over Joseph's orchards, apple and pomegranate, palm and fig, in the shade of whose leafy branches were many wild birds, sparrow and wagtail and dove. But for these, and the bell-clear sound of running water and the stir of the servants who came and went, all was still and tranquil, and the air was cool and sweet.

When Joseph's brothers, who stood waiting beside their asses in the courtyard, knew that this was the palace of the great lord himself, they were abashed and filled with mistrust. They murmured one to another: "It is for no good of ours that we have been brought hither. It must be because of the money that was put back secretly into our sacks. It is a device to betray us. We are alone and defenceless. This great lord will accuse us falsely; his servants will fall upon us, and seize all that we have. We are doomed."

While the others thus waited in grievous trouble of mind at what might come of it, two of them went to the entry of the house and asked if they might speak with the steward.

"Sir," they said, when he came to them, "we entreat thee to think no evil of us. We are, as you know, from the land of Canaan, and strangers here, and we have merely journeyed down again into Egypt as we did before, and as we were bidden, to buy corn because of the famine. When we were sent away after our first coming here, we found when we unladed our asses that the money we had brought with us had been restored to us and hidden in our sacks—the money we had actually paid for the corn. Nor have we any inkling of how this came about. But we have brought it back with us, with other money to buy food, and here it is."

Joseph's steward answered them courteously and reassured them: "All is well. There is nothing to fear. Surely it cannot but have been the will of your God, and of the God of your fathers, that this treasure came to be hidden in your sacks? Of my own knowledge you paid the full price for your corn, and I have a record to prove it so."

Then he brought Simeon to them, and himself led them within to where they could refresh themselves and prepare for the coming of Joseph. He gave them water to wash their feet, and their asses were fed and watered. There, with hearts renewed, they made ready the present they had brought with them, the aromatic gums and spices, the honey and pistachio nuts, for they had heard that Joseph would be returning at noon, and that they were to eat with him. They talked eagerly among themselves, marvelling at the splendour and strangeness of Joseph's house, and wondering what was in store for them after the kindness that had been shown to them by the steward.

When Joseph came home, they were taken into his presence; and they bowed themselves and made obeisance. And they presented him with the gifts which they had brought with them from Canaan. And Joseph in thanking them almost betrayed himself in his speech. The old words of delight evoked by a thousand memories sprang into his mind as he saw the familiar plaited baskets and breathed in the fragrance of the spices. But he stayed himself, and through his interpreter asked them of their welfare. "Is your father," he said, "the old man of whom you spoke to me, still alive, and in good health?"

"Thy servant our father", they said, "is still alive and is well."

Looking from one to the other, Joseph's eyes rested at last on the face of his brother Benjamin, his own loved mother's son.

"Is this, then," he said, "the younger brother whom you told me of? You have done well to bring him with you."

He gazed long at Benjamin. "May God", he said, "be gracious unto thee, my son." But the words faltered on his lips, and he turned away in haste, for his heart yearned for Benjamin and he could not keep back his tears. He went into his own chamber alone, and wept there. And when he had grown calmer, he rose and washed his face, and returned to them again, restraining himself.

He signed to his steward that the feast should be served,

and the whole company gathered there sat down to eat. His own place at the feast was set apart by reason of his dignity and lordship in Egypt. His officers and attendants and other guests also sate together apart; for the Egyptians might not eat of the same dish with the Hebrews; it was forbidden by their priests and their religion.

As for his brothers, Joseph himself arranged the order in which they should sit before him, from Reuben, the first-born, according to his birthright, to Benjamin, the youngest, according to his youth. At this they gazed at one another in astonishment, marvelling how he had divined their ages, for he had seated them in order of age without a single mistake. And now the feast began. The air was sweet with the fragrance of flowers. There were fruits and meats and wines in all abundance, and they drank out of goblets of glass, a thing they had never seen before.

And as was the custom in Egypt, Joseph chose from the dishes set before him, and sent them by the hands of his servants to his brothers—honouring them as his guests. But the dainties he sent to Benjamin were five times as many as to any of the others; and they ate and drank and feasted with Joseph, and were merry.

And while they sate feasting, Joseph spoke with his steward. "Let these men's sacks", he said, "be filled with corn to the utmost their beasts can carry. And in the sack of the youngest of them—whom you see yonder—put in also the money that was paid for his corn, and hide therein my cup—my silver divining cup. But all this in secret! Let not a rumour of it reach their ears." And the steward did as Joseph had bidden him.

As soon as it was light next morning, Joseph's brothers set out on their journey home; and a joyful and merry-hearted company they were. It seemed that everything was now well with them, their troubles over, Benjamin safe, and Simeon restored to them.

But soon after they were gone, and before they had proceeded far beyond the outskirts of the city, Joseph called for his steward. "Up now," he said. "Away, and with all speed! Take a guard of soldiers with thee and follow hard after these Hebrews, and when thou hast overtaken them, bid them stand, and accuse them openly: 'Why have you returned evil for good? My lord's silver cup has been stolen, even the cup which he uses for divination. He knows of a certainty into whose hands it has fallen, and that that thief is one on whom but yesterday he lavished many kindnesses. What wickedness could be viler!' "

The steward did as he was bid. He took a guard of soldiers, and mounting a camel, rode out in hot haste after them, and overtook them in the desert before yet the sun was high in the heavens. When at sound of pursuit the brothers turned and looked back, they instantly fell silent, and their hearts stood still for dread. They drew up immediately and clustered together about him, in horror of what new disaster was now upon them. The steward challenged them harshly. He upbraided them as if they were outcasts beneath contempt, and he repeated everything that Joseph had bidden him. They gazed one at another in confusion; a cold and awful darkness had fallen upon them.

"God forbid", they said, "that we should have been guilty of such a thing, or that my lord should so much as have thought it of us. Did we not ourselves tell you of the money which after our first journey we found in our sacks, and did we not offer it you again only yesterday? And you said: 'All's well, be at peace, for God has ordained it so'. What need have we of silver or gold that we should return evil for good and rob thy lord himself? And now you even accuse us of having stolen his divining cup! Search as you please, and if the goblet be found in the sack of any one of us, then let him die; and the rest of us shall be bondsmen of thy lord from this day onward."

Then said the steward: "Be it as you say; except that only the one of you in whose sack the cup is found shall suffer, for he alone is guilty. The rest being blameless shall go free."

They unloaded their asses, put their sacks on the ground, and loosed the thongs that bound their mouths. Then, beginning with that of the eldest of them, the steward and his guard searched their sacks one by one until at length they came to the sack of the youngest, Benjamin. There the cup was found, and his money beside it.

At sight of it his brothers rent their clothes in woe and despair. Their darkest premonitions had come true. They knew what fate awaited them, that all was lost. But one and all of them refrained from uttering a word of reproach or making the least sign, by frown or gesture, that they blamed Benjamin or misdoubted his innocence.

They tied up their sacks, loaded up their asses again, and turned back in wretchedness towards the city by the way they had come. Though again and again, as Joseph had bidden him, the steward assured them that it was only the thief himself his lord intended to punish, they refused to have any further word with him and made no answer. With Benjamin in their midst, they made haste to return.

Joseph was seated in his hall of audience amid his officers. He raised his eyes and surveyed them. They flung themselves down before him, their faces to the earth. But he hardened his face and addressed them scornfully and as if in anger.

"What deed is this that you have done? Knew you not that I could divine the truth in this matter?"

Then Judah spoke in answer for them all. "What shall we say unto my lord? How shall I speak? Of what use are words to clear ourselves from a charge so black against us, yet one of which we are wholly innocent? That, my lord, is the truth. But doubtless the judgment of God has fallen upon us not for this evil of which we are innocent, but for the wickedness we have done in the past. We are strangers in a strange land, and have none to defend us. We cannot even speak in a tongue that might persuade my lord to listen. We can but cast ourselves upon the mercy of my lord, and if he so will it, let him make bondsmen of us all, so that we suffer together, and not alone."

And Joseph answered: "God forbid that I should do so! It is known to me which among you was found in possession of the cup. He alone is guilty, and he alone shall suffer. As for the rest of you, there is nothing to keep you here; get you gone in peace, then, while you may. Return to your father in Canaan and let me see your faces no more."

Then Judah drew near to him and spoke earnestly with him face to face, telling him everything that was in his heart and keeping nothing back.

"Oh, my lord," he said, "let thy servant, I pray thee, tell out everything that is in his mind. Have patience, and let not thine anger burn against thy servant, for thou art all-powerful, even as Pharaoh himself. When first we came into Egypt—I myself and these men, my brothers—to buy corn, my lord questioned us, who we were and whence we had come, and who our father was, and were we his only sons. And we told my lord: we have a father, who is now an old man. We said that there was one son remaining with him, a child of his old age, dearest to him of us all, and the only son left of his mother, his brother being dead.

"And my lord gave command to his servants: 'Go and return and bring back with you this brother of whom you speak that I may see him with my own eyes.' And we told my lord, the lad cannot leave his father, for if he should, and any harm came to him, his father would die. And my lord said expressly to his servants: 'Unless your youngest brother come down with you into Egypt, and that soon, you shall see my face no more.'

"Well, my lord, when we came up unto thy servant our father, we laid before him all that my lord had said. And the time came when our need being extreme because of the famine, he bade us come again and buy a little food. We answered that we could not do this unless our youngest brother went with us, since without him we should not even be admitted into my lord's presence. And our father said: 'Why did you so much as mention your youngest brother? You knew well how dearly I love him. You knew that he is the only son left to me of his mother who is dead. Long, long ago his brother, young and happy, bade me farewell and set out upon a journey from which he never returned. It may be that he was torn to pieces by wild beasts. And now you would take his younger brother also, knowing well that if any harm befall him, you will bring down my grey hairs in sorrow to the grave.'

"Oh, my lord, my father's life itself is bound up with this lad's safety. If I return without him and he look for him and find him not, surely his grief will be greater than he can bear; and it is we ourselves, his own sons, that shall have brought down this grey-haired old man with sorrow to the grave. And I myself, alas, shall be the most to blame, for I vowed solemnly to my father to take every care of him. 'If', I said, 'I bring him not back unharmed and in safety, then the blame be mine for ever!'

"I beseech thee, then, my lord, have pity. Let the lad go free, and return home with his brothers, and let me be bondsman in his stead. My lord, I could not bear to return without him and see my father's grief."

Joseph heard him in silence to the end; glancing from one to another of his brothers, as they stood in fear and disgrace before him, and letting his eyes rest on Benjamin, who was a little apart from them, not daring to lift his head for shame that he should have been thought guilty of stealing the cup. And when Judah spoke of his father, and there

returned into Joseph's mind all that had passed since he had
seen him, he could refrain himself no longer.

"Let every man", he said, "withdraw out of my presence,
except only these Hebrews."

When Joseph's officers and attendants all were gone and
there stood no man with him except his brothers, he came
down to them and made himself known to them. And he
wept, so that even the Egyptians who lingered on the
threshold heard him weeping.

And he said to his brothers: "Come near, I pray you.
There is nothing now to fear. For see, I am Joseph—Joseph
himself, who long ago you thought was dead. Tell me, I beseech you, is indeed all well with my father? Is he truly yet
alive?"

But his brothers were troubled at his presence, gazing at
him in dismay, and could make no answer.

Joseph smiled at them: "It is no wonder", he said, "after
the many years we have been separated one from another
that you should still be in doubt of who I am. But come now,
look closely at me, for I am indeed and in truth none other
than Joseph, the very Joseph whom you sold to the Ishmaelites and into Egypt. Be no more distressed or angry
with yourselves because of that. God sent me on before you
so that in this time of need I might preserve your lives, for
else you might have perished for want. For two years now
there has been famine in Egypt. But five years are yet to
come when there will be drought and bitter scarcity, and
want and suffering must increase. Take comfort, then; remember only that it was God in his mercy who made me
the means of this deliverance and of saving not only yourselves, but your children and your children's children, who
will follow us when we are gone. I say, then, it was not you
who sent me hither, but God. It is he alone who hath given

me power under Pharaoh to act as seems best to me—lord of his house and viceroy of all Egypt. Hasten then and return with all the speed you can to my father. Give him this message in these same words: 'I myself, thy long-lost son, Joseph, am awaiting thee here in Egypt, pining to see thee again, anxious only for thy health and safety.'

"Say that, and tell my father also that you have seen me face to face, even as I am; and that the God of whom he taught me as a child has made me lord and ruler over all the land of Egypt. Entreat him not to delay, but to return with you into Egypt. A place shall be found for him and for you all where you shall live near me and under my protection, you and your wives and your children, your flocks and herds, and all that you have. Through all the evils that are yet to come I myself will provide for him and for you all, and will cherish his last years lest he should come to poverty."

As he stood in their midst, his words followed one upon another out of his inmost heart like water welling from a long-sealed fountain. And his face was lighted with his love.

But still they dared make no sign, or, after so many vicissitudes, trust even their own senses. They gazed and were silent.

"But, no?" he said, smiling. "I see you are still in doubt. Well, then, Benjamin your youngest and my own dear mother's son shall tell you what I say is true, that it is my own mouth that speaks to you, and that I am indeed his brother Joseph."

And he took Benjamin into his arms and fell upon his neck and kissed him, and in love and joy wept upon his shoulder.

Seeing this, the rest of them were at last reassured and believed him. They drew near and he kissed them all in turn.

After that they talked together for a long time in private there, for there was much to hear and much to tell. There were no bounds to their happiness.

Jacob Comes Down into Egypt

When Joseph's steward and the officers of his household heard what had come about, they too rejoiced. And it was told Pharaoh himself that after many years of separation, Joseph's own brethren had come into Egypt to buy corn, and had at first not recognized him or even so much as dreamed it was he; but that he had now made himself known to them and they were reunited. This pleased Pharaoh well, and he himself spoke with Joseph.

"Tell your brethren", he said, "that it is Pharaoh's will and desire that they return at once into their own country and bring back with them your father and their wives and children. Bid them trouble not with what goods they have. For from henceforth they shall have the best that Egypt affords, they shall live on the fat of the land and shall never again be in want or danger. Let them be supplied with baggage-wagons and with whatever else they may need in their long and arduous journey into Egypt—for themselves, their wives and their little ones and for your father. Thou knowest that in all things thy joys are my joys. Let nothing then be wanting for their comfort and for thine own peace of mind. The best that Egypt has is theirs."

So Joseph gave orders that his brothers should be provided with baggage-wagons as Pharaoh had said, with horses to draw them, and beasts of burden, and all things else and every comfort that his father or their wives and their daughters might need on the journey.

For presents, too, from himself, he gave them one and all changes of raiment, the choicest in Egypt, famous through the ages for the fineness of its linen. But to his brother Benjamin he gave three hundred pieces of silver and five changes of raiment. To his father he sent a present too, such as prince might send to prince—ten he-asses laden with all the riches of Egypt—things of beauty, rare and costly; and ten she-asses, their paniers piled with wheat and fruits and delicacies for his comfort on the journey.

The next morning, when they were assembled together in the courtyard of Joseph's house, and beyond its gates stood ready the baggage-wagons and the asses and the servants that were to go with them, Joseph himself came down out of his house to greet them and to bid them farewell; and his two small sons were with him. He embraced his brothers, and gave them but one word of counsel. "Remember only this," he said, "that between you and me there remains nothing now but love and friendship, so let there be peace between you all. No reproaches, no recriminations, nothing but well and fair until we meet again. I would not that you fall out with one another by the way."

They talked together until the last moment came for their departure. Their cares were over, and as they set out in the clear brightness of the morning a great company of Joseph's household watched them go.

Day after day they continued on their journey, sleeping when dark came on where it was customary for caravans to camp for the night, until, after they had turned inward from the sea, they came without mischance into Canaan. News had already been brought to Jacob from servants whom he had sent out to keep watch for them, that they were drawing near. They came together to his tent, and when he saw that Simeon was with them, and Benjamin himself was clasped again in his arms, he bowed his head in thanks to God for this great mercy.

Hope had all but faded into despair; now he was at peace. But when they told him that his son Joseph was not only still alive but was lord and governor over the whole land of Egypt, he gazed at them trembling. His heart fainted within him; for joy itself may be so sudden sweet as to be beyond credence. He could not believe them. He sat gazing mutely into their faces, and they were filled with remorse.

Even when they repeated to him in Joseph's own words the message he had bidden them bring, his mind was still in confusion. It was not until, supporting his feeble footsteps, they led him out, and with his own eyes he saw the Egyptian wagons, and the horses that had been sent to carry him into Egypt, that he doubted no more. His spirit revived within him.

"It is enough," he said. "Joseph my son is yet alive: I will go and see him before I die."

As Pharaoh the King had expressly decreed, preparations were now speedily made to leave for ever the Vale of Hebron—now parched dry as bone with the long drought —in which they had dwelt peacefully so many years. They gathered together all that remained of their flocks and herds, and loaded their beasts of burden with their tents, their clothes and all the goods they had gotten in the land of Canaan.

On the day appointed, before even break of dawn, their little ones were up and ready; wild with delight and expectation. They mounted up into the Egyptian wagons—

and the mothers with their babies. They marvelled at the
horses of Pharaoh and their caparisons of gilded leather.
The sun rose; the dew-mists thinned away. The cry of the
drivers sounded, and the crack of whip. The horses strained
at their traces. With the bright clothes of the children in the
wagons, and their smiling faces, it was as though great
heaps of nodding flowers were in motion, as in the first of
morning the happy multitude began to set forward. The
fresh windless air rang with their talk and laughter, with
the bleating of sheep, the lowing of cattle and their sheep-
dogs' barking; and a great dust rose into the sky, beaten up
by hoof and wheel, and gently descended again after they
had gone by.

And so they came to Beersheba, the southernmost city of Canaan, which few among them were to see again. There they pitched camp, and rested, and there Jacob offered sacrifices to the Lord and poured out his heart in thankfulness for his great mercy. It was the place where he was born.

That night as he lay asleep there came to him a vision; and in dream he heard a voice calling him: "Jacob! Jacob!" And he knew in his dream that it was the voice of God.

He answered: "Lord, here am I."

And the voice said:

"I am thy God and the God of thy fathers, and I will never forsake thee whithersoever thou goest. Fear not to go down into Egypt. There I will make of thee and of thy sons a great nation. And thy children's children shall return and possess this Canaan that thou lovest. Here thou thyself shalt find thy last resting-place, and thy son Joseph shall lay his hand upon thine eyes and give thee peace in thy long sleep."

And Jacob awoke from his dream, and was comforted.

The next day Judah was sent on ahead of the cavalcade to inquire of Joseph where they should pitch their tents when, their journey over, they had come down by the sea coast into Egypt. And, as Pharaoh had ordained, they went up into the land of Goshen which lay a little northward, between the Lake of the Crocodiles and the great river. It was a region richer in good pasturage than any other in Egypt. As soon as word was brought of their safe arrival, Joseph made ready his chariot, and with his officers and his bodyguard, he rode out in state to welcome his father and to show him honour.

It was evening when he drew near. He alighted from his chariot and approached on foot, and presented himself to his father in the entering-in of his tent where he stood waiting to receive him. Jacob was now bent and feeble with age, but his face lit with rapture at sight of Joseph, as in the radiance of the declining sun he bowed himself low before his father. He put his arms about Joseph's neck and embraced him. And he wept upon his shoulder, and there was a long silence between them. Then he tenderly drew back Joseph's face and gazed into it in joy and love, and he said: "My son, my son! Life hath nothing more to give me. Now let me die; for I have seen thy face again and know that thou art still in the land of the living."

They talked together for many hours alone. Then Joseph bade his father farewell for a season, though they were soon to meet again, and he returned to his own house. He took with him five of his brothers, and presented them to Pharaoh, each of them by name. They bowed themselves and made obeisance, and Pharaoh conversed with them by means of an interpreter, questioning them concerning the condition of the country of Canaan from which they had come, and their lives and their occupations.

They told Pharaoh that the famine was still very grievous in Canaan, that there was little hope of respite, and that had it not been for the corn they had been enabled to buy in Egypt, they would have perished at last of hunger and want. "For we ourselves are shepherds," they said, "and depend on our flocks as our fathers did before us." They spoke with grateful hearts of the land of Goshen; praising it for the richness of its pasturage and its abundance of water for their sheep and their goats.

When they were gone out from the presence of the king, Pharaoh spoke alone with Joseph.

He said: "Let thy brethren remain in the land of Goshen; they shall dwell there in peace and security. It is a region like this Hebron, it seems, of which they tell me, and if there be among them any that have knowledge and skill in the keeping of cattle, let my herds be given into their charge. They shall be made overseers over my herdsmen and be responsible to me for them. And now, tell me, is thy father safe and well after so long a journey?"

And Joseph brought Jacob his father into the presence of Pharaoh. The old man raised his trembling hands in salutation of the king and blessed him. And Pharaoh inquired of him concerning his life and of his long experience in this world. He asked him: "How old art thou?"

And Jacob answered the king: "The days of my pilgrimage on earth are now a hundred and thirty years. Few and evil have they been when I reflect on them. I have not attained, nor shall I attain, to the age of my father and of his father before him. For my life has seen little rest from wandering, and my griefs have been many."

Pharaoh spoke very graciously to the old man and with all the courtesy and reverence due to his grey hairs and to one who had endured so many sorrows.

So, as Pharaoh had decreed, Jacob and his household with all his children and grandchildren settled in the land of Goshen. There they lived in peace. And Joseph watched over them like a father whose one care is the safety and comfort of his little ones. He supplied all their needs, and they wanted for nothing.

But in Egypt—as in Canaan—while still the great river refused its fostering waters, the famine increased in severity, until apart from the grain in the royal granaries, there was no bread in all the land, and only by Joseph's wisdom and forethought were the people saved from perishing in misery and starvation. The money they paid for their corn was amassed in the treasuries of the king, and his wealth was beyond all computation. And when their money had been expended, they were compelled to barter their cattle, their horses, their flocks, and their asses, in exchange merely for bread, so sharp and extreme was the famine.

These gone, they had nothing but the service of their own bodies and the land they owned to offer in payment. Wherefore they sold their land to the king for corn and for seed. And when the granaries of one district were exhausted Joseph removed the people that dwelt there to some other region of Egypt, where there still remained supplies of grain sufficient for them. Even after the years of famine were over, the people continued to lease their lands from the king, and for rent paid into the royal treasury one-fifth of their annual harvest, except only the priests of Egypt who were under the personal protection of Pharaoh, and who were provided with all that they needed out of his royal bounty.

For seventeen years Jacob lived on in the land of Goshen. His sons prospered and had great possessions there. And the family of Israel grew and multiplied. But there came a day when he was so enfeebled with age and sickness that he knew his earthly pilgrimage would soon be at an end, and that he must die.

Message was sent to Joseph that his father was sick unto death. He came in haste to see him, bringing with him his two sons, Ephraim and Manasseh. The women that were waiting upon his father in the tent withdrew. The old man lay upon his bed, as if asleep. In sorrow beyond speech, Joseph knelt down beside him and laid his hand in caress upon the wasted hand of his father. His eyes opened; he gazed into Joseph's face and smiled, as if all his troubles were now ended.

"Thou hast come," he said. "It is enough. There is little

time left to me, my son, but I have one urgent thing to ask of thee. If peradventure I have found grace in thy sight, I entreat thee that in the last thou wilt deal kindly and truly with me, and bury me not in Egypt, where I am a stranger, but carry me again into Canaan, the land of my fathers. There and with them let me lie at rest in the burial place that is prepared for me."

Joseph gazed into the wasted face. "Whatsoever thou mayst ask of me, that in truth will I do."

And Jacob said: "Nay, I entreat thee, let it be a vow between thee and me, my son, for it is matter very near to my heart."

Joseph sware unto him, and his father was greatly comforted. Strength returned into him. He raised himself in his bed and thanked God that he was now at peace.

Then Joseph brought his two sons into the presence of his father. They stood within the entry, tarrying until he should call them near.

But Jacob's eyes were dim and he looked at them without recognition. "Who are these?" he said.

"These are my two sons", said Joseph, "whom thou knowest well. They were given me of God in Egypt, and are come to ask thy blessing."

He led them by the hand and brought them to the bedside, and his father stretched out his hand and laid his right hand on Ephraim's head and his left hand on Manasseh's, and he did this wittingly though he knew that Manasseh was Joseph's firstborn. For in the light of death he foresaw that in years to come the descendants of the younger would exceed those of the elder in greatness and numbers. And he blessed them and embraced them.

He reminded Joseph how the Lord God had appeared to him in a vision in the night when he lay sleeping in the wilds of Bethel, and how he had made known to him that those who came after him should inherit the land of Canaan for an everlasting inheritance.

"Very dear was thy mother Rachel to me, my son, but when we were journeying from Bethel but a little distance from Ephrath near Bethlehem, she died at the wayside. I mourned and wept over her, and there I buried her. How then could I else but love thee very dearly also, thee and thy brother Benjamin? So, too, these thy sons, whom thou lovest, shall be remembered, and they shall partake of the glories of Israel when it has become a nation and is entered into the land that God hath promised. For many long and weary years I had not thought to see thy face again, and now behold God hath not only restored thee to me, but hath given me breath to bless thy two sons also."

And Ephraim and Manasseh bowed themselves before the bed and withdrew. When Joseph was again alone with his father he watched beside him, and between his fitful slumbers they communed together.

"Behold I die," said Jacob, "but God shall be with thee."

And Joseph stooped himself, weeping, beside the bed, and kissed his father, and Jacob gave him his last blessing.

Then the rest of his sons came together into his presence and he blessed them one and all, predicting with his last words what the future would bring forth for all that came after them, their children's children for unnumbered generations. For though the shadows of death were darkening over him, his mind was clear and his vision untroubled. With this he bade them a last farewell, and composed himself to die. He drew his feet up into the bed, yielded up his spirit to God who gave it, and was gathered to his people.

When Joseph saw that life was gone, he prostrated himself beside his father, kissed him and wept over him, and remained with him in death, alone, in bitter grief.

Then to the physicians who were in his service, men skilled in the embalming of the dead, he entrusted the body of his father, and they embalmed it with precious salts and spices and swathed it in the finest linen. And not only Jacob's sons and their households mourned for him, but Pharaoh himself, his chief counsellors and his whole court and the Egyptians throughout Egypt, from the highest to the lowest, mourned for him also. Seventy days was the period of Egypt's mourning for this stranger, for the story of how Joseph, Pharaoh's renowned vizier, had as by a wonder been restored to his father and to his brethren long after he had been given up for dead, was known throughout the whole country, from one end of it to the other.

And Joseph made known to Pharaoh that he had solemnly sworn to his father that his body should be buried not in Egypt, since it was a country strange to him, but in the land of Canaan, where he was born, and in the tomb of Isaac his father.

"Give me leave, I pray thee, then," he said, "to absent myself from Egypt a while, that I may keep the vow I made to my father when he was nearing death and may bury him in the place where he himself desired to rest. Then will I return again." And Pharaoh consented.

A very great company went up out of Egypt to Jacob's burial, for not only Joseph himself with his brothers and all their households, except only their little ones, followed his father to the grave, but also the chief officers of Pharaoh's palace, the governors of the cities of Egypt, and the stewards whom Joseph had appointed over the granaries. There went with them also an escort of many chariots and a multitude of horsemen.

When this great concourse had come into Canaan, to the threshing-floor of Atad that was beyond Jordan, the mourners who followed after the gilded coffin containing the embalmed body of Jacob, lifted up their voices and made lament with dirges and wailings. There Joseph and the lords of Egypt that were with him mourned for his father seven days.

When the people of Canaan who dwelt near the Jordan heard this great mourning and lamentation, they marvelled. "Of a surety," they said, one to another, "this must be a day of sore sorrow and bitterness to the Egyptians."

And afterwards, Joseph and his brethren went on alone and the body of their father was laid to rest beside his father

Isaac, in the tomb hewn out of the rock at Machpelah, which Abraham, Isaac's father, had himself purchased and prepared for his own burial-place. Then Joseph and all who had accompanied him into Canaan returned into Egypt.

The funeral pomp and ceremonies of the Egyptians, and the great cavalcade that had gone up with them into Canaan were to his brothers a fresh revelation of Joseph's sovran power in the land. And when they were alone together again, mere shepherds and overseers of cattle, they were seized with misgivings.

The fear had suddenly come upon them that maybe it was only while their father was still alive that Joseph had refrained from requiting them for all the evil they had done against him; that through the years which had gone by he had been merely concealing his hatred of them, biding his time; and that now the day had come when his full vengeance would sweep down upon them.

A messenger was sent; for they feared to see him. By him they made known to Joseph that when their father was lying sick to death they themselves confessed their act of lying treachery against him, after they had sold Joseph to the Ishmaelites.

"And he himself charged us before he died", they said, "to give thee this message. 'Say unto my beloved son Joseph,' he said, 'forgive, I pray thee, the evil which thy brothers did against thee, and all the misery that came of it.' We entreat thee then to heed the words of our father and of thy father, and to forgive us the evils of which we were guilty against the God he worshipped."

Joseph was distressed that they mistrusted him. He at once sent for them all, and they were brought into his presence where he sat alone. They prostrated themselves before him and made obeisance as of old.

"Behold," they said, "we are the servants of the God of thy father. Do with us as seems best to thee."

And Joseph reassured them. It grieved him to the heart to see them humbling themselves before him.

"Put away your fears," he said. "Think you that I stand here in God's stead to judge and punish whom I may? Surely it is not so. For even though in the days that are gone and best forgotten you did me this injury, it was his will that only good should come of it. For by this I was made the means of saving you and your wives and your little ones and many another from death itself. Put away all your cares then, and think no more of them, either now or at any time in the future. Believe only that it is my one hope and desire to protect you and your little ones, and to watch over you, lest being among strangers in a strange land you should come to any harm."

He comforted them and spoke kindly to them, saying all that was in his heart, and they doubted him no more.

So Joseph continued to dwell in Egypt, and they with him. He lived long enough to see around him his son Ephraim's grandchildren, and the children also of Machir, the son of Manasseh. Even when he was a very old man, these little ones would be brought in to see him, for he loved children. And they would sit talking to him upon his knee.

But the day came when he knew that death was approaching. And he sent for his brothers to bid them farewell.

"I am dying", he said, "and these must be my last words to you; bear them, I pray you, in mind. God will surely be ever with you, and in his own season will bring those who come after you up out of Egypt and into the land which he promised to Abraham, to Isaac, and to our father Jacob, even into Canaan. In that day may I myself be remembered, as may God remember you. Vow unto me then that my bones shall be carried up hence and laid to rest beside my father." And they swore it to him.

And Joseph died, being a hundred and ten years old. And his physicians and embalmers embalmed his body and laid it in a coffin, and his coffin was enshrined in a sarcophagus of rich and strange and curious workmanship, and this was given into the charge of his brethren in Goshen. And Pharaoh the king and all his court and the whole land of Egypt sorrowed and mourned for Joseph many days, for of all the king's counsellors none in foresight, divination, power and wisdom, had been greater than he.

MOSES

The Ark of Bulrushes

Now Jacob was called Israel. He was the son of Isaac, whose father was Abraham, the servant of God. And these are the names of Jacob's sons that came down with him out of Canaan into Egypt: Reuben, Simeon, Levi, Judah, Issachar, Zebulun, Dan, Naphtali, Gad, Asher and Benjamin. With their households, their wives and their children, seventy souls of Jacob's blood in all, with their servants and herdsmen and handmaids, they came down, and set up their tents in the rich pastures of Goshen, a land east of Egypt, and west of what were then the northern reaches of the Red Sea. And a shallow cultivated strip of land, watered by a canal, stretched out east again of Goshen towards this sea.

There, as long as Joseph lived, and in his loving favour and protection, they dwelt. There they prospered, following the peaceful life of shepherds. And to some of them was deputed the charge of the king's cattle. They were the keepers of Pharaoh's herds.

As time went on, they died, and all their kindred and all that generation. But their children's children who had been born and reared in Egypt, and their descendants also, increased so abundantly that in the centuries that followed they spread abroad throughout the whole region of Goshen. They became a nation. The land was filled with them.

They too continued to prosper. But there came at length

a day when a new king arose in Egypt—a king to whom the
name and fame of Joseph was naught. He was a man of a
rare personal beauty and renowned for his valour. He
reigned for many years, and in power and conquest was one
of the mightiest monarchs that ever sat on the throne of
Egypt. He led his armies to victory in Syria, in Libya, and
in Nubia. He besieged Khetesh, the chief city of the Hit-
tites, on the island in the midst of the river Orontes, and
utterly subdued them. He built vast solemn temples to the
gods of Egypt, rich in splendour and treasure, himself both
priest and king. The avenue of sphinxes, man-headed lions
of stone, which he caused to be made, his prodigious pylons
or gateways, the granite image of himself towering above
thirty cubits in stature from its headdress to its foot, and
the records of his victories incised in the stones of his monu-
ments—all these continue for earthly record of him to this
day.

But he knew not Joseph. The services that as viceroy
Joseph had rendered to Egypt in the seven years when its
harvests failed and when by his insight and wisdom he had
saved its people from famine and death, had been forgotten. In the eyes of this Pharaoh the Hebrews in Goshen
were no longer a favoured people under his special grace.
He regarded them with suspicion and distrust.

They occupied territory on the most dangerous frontier
of Egypt. He saw how rapidly they grew in power and
numbers—a race of alien blood and customs and religion,
and, though small in stature, keen and alert in body and
mind. And he feared that a day might come when Egypt
being at war, they might ally themselves with his enemies
and, fighting against him, fling off his domination over
them and become a free people. His distrust poisoned his
mind against them; and when the campaigns beyond his

borders no longer occupied his mind, he took counsel on the matter with his chief statesmen and advisers.

"These Hebrews", he said, "have become a danger and a menace, and if nothing be done to keep them in subjection, they will swarm like flies among us to such a degree that they will become more numerous than the Egyptians themselves. Let us so deal with them, then, as to give them neither the power nor temptation to revolt and to betray us."

He set over them masters of works or overseers, men who would enforce his orders with a high hand. These overseers divided Goshen into districts, and the Hebrews who dwelt in them into droves or gangs. They were each of them responsible for a certain district; and over every gang they appointed a foreman who was himself a Hebrew. They spared no man either on account of his youth or age or infirmity—all must serve the king.

Little by little they increased the labour they exacted from the Hebrews until they had reduced them to a state of cruel bondage from which there was no release. They brought down their lives to a continual hardship, compelling them to toil like beasts of burden, driven on by rod and lash, until, worn to skin and bone, they could work no more, and were flung aside to die.

They cut canals and built dams, by means of which the waters of the great river of Egypt were heaped up to higher levels for the irrigation of the soil. They dug ditches and made conduits, and raised water from one conduit to another by means of buckets fixed to a pole hung upon an axle between two posts—filling and emptying, filling and emptying from morn to eve, to water the Egyptians' crops, to replenish their fish-ponds, and flush the conduits in their gardens and orchards.

In the glare and heat of the sun they laboured all day in

the desert quarries. They hewed and cut and dragged away over wooden rollers or on sleds huge ponderous blocks of marble and granite to serve for the building of Pharaoh's temples to the strange gods of Egypt. For monument and sculpture also—gigantic images and obelisks fretted with hieroglyphs proclaiming the valour, glory and wisdom of the king.

But for the most part these slave-gangs were set to the making of bricks. Some dug out the silt or mud. Others carried water in their water-jars from the tanks or cisterns to moisten it. Yet others kneaded the mud, trampling it with their feet until it was smooth and fit for use, and mixing with it chopped-up straw to bind it together. The more skilled among them then shaped the mud thus prepared by forcing it into great sanded moulds stamped within with the symbol of the king.

The bricks thus shaped, while still soft, were carried off on a framework of wood, slung from a yoke over the shoulders, and were stacked in rows one above the other, with chinks for air between them, and straw to prevent them from sticking together. There they lay until they were baked dry and black in the blazing heat of the sun.

Such were the labours of the Hebrews—the men of Israel—under Pharaoh, which they were compelled to endure without complaint; wageless, hopeless and ill-fed. Yet, the more ruthlessly they were oppressed and afflicted, the more they increased in numbers and the further they spread. The Egyptians came to look on them with loathing and contempt.

Seeing at last that no toil or hardship he had devised could keep them in subjection, Pharaoh decreed that of all the children born to the women of the Hebrews only their daughters should be allowed to live. Their sons, their men-children, were to be snatched away at birth from their mothers' breasts, and flung into the Nile. As he commanded, so it was done. There was lamentation and weeping in Goshen. And for this, beyond all else, the people of Israel feared and hated Pharaoh and his overseers; but were powerless to revolt.

None the less and in spite of this decree there came about the deliverance of Israel; for the Lord raised up a leader among them whose name has been famous throughout the ages and to this day.

There was a woman of the family of Levi whose name was Jochabed. She was a widow when her husband had taken her to wife, and she already had two children, a daughter named Miriam, and a son, but three years old, called Aaron. She was of a lively and fearless spirit, and when a second son was born to her, she hid him away. He was fair in face beyond any child in Israel, strong and comely, and she counted her own life as nothing so long as he was safe. For three whole months she nursed and tended him and kept him hidden, though every passing footfall and his least little cry filled her with terror that her secret might be discovered.

When she could hide him no longer, she began to think within herself what she should do to keep him safe. And there came a bold device into her mind. She went down one evening to the brink of the river, and gathered there a bundle of the long flowery-tufted reeds or bulrushes that grew in its shallows. Of these she made a little ark or coffer or jonket, hollow within and rounded without, and woven close. And she plaited a roof or lid to it, on a hinge.

When the ark had been securely woven together in the fashion of basket-makers, she daubed it over with silt and pitch to make it water-tight, even as long ages before had been the great ark of Noah himself; and she left it to dry.

As soon as it was light the next morning, and while the stars were yet faint in the sky, she rose up, and having fed the child and done all that was needful for his comfort, she lulled him into a deep and quiet sleep again, and kissed him, and put him into the ark and covered him over with the roof of rushes which she had woven to shield him from the heat of the sun. Then, with her daughter Miriam, she stole off down to the river, no-one by, and hid the ark among the nodding water-weeds at its brink. Having made sure that it would float in safety where it lay, she left her small daughter to keep watch over it, and herself returned home. The child then hid herself among the reeds and rushes where she could keep the ark continually in sight.

The birds flitted back to their haunts; only their trillings and the lapping of the water and the sighing and whisper of the reeds broke the hush. The hours sped softly on, and nothing had come to alarm or disturb the child when of a sudden she heard the sound of voices sweet and clear. She peered out of her hiding-place and, scarcely able to breathe, drew swiftly back again.

For, behold, it was the daughter of Pharaoh the King whose voice she had heard, and who with her maidens was come down to the river to bathe. Presently after, still laughing and talking, her maidens withdrew; and, fair themselves as lotus flowers, strayed along by the water-side gathering lilies, while, with none but her own handmaid to attend upon her, this princess, the daughter of Pharaoh, prepared to bathe.

On drawing near to the river in her naked loveliness, she looked and saw there the ark hidden among the reeds, black but glinting in the sun, and rocked gently to and fro upon the rippled water. She stayed, wondering, and, with the palm of her hand above her eyes, steadfastly watched a while, in doubt of what this strange object could be. Then she bade her handmaid wade into the water and bring it in.

This she did. Lifting up the ark in her arms from out of the water, she carried it to her mistress, and she herself lifted its lid. And there, mantled up softly within, its cheeks flushed with sleep, was a little child, which, as soon as the bright beams of the sun pierced into the narrow darkness wherein it lay, stirred in its slumbers, awoke and wept. The daughter of Pharaoh stooped, and taking the child into her arms, nestled it to her breast, and soothed its fears.

At sound of her gentle voice it looked up into her face and stayed its weeping; and with the tears yet wet upon its cheek, thrust out a hand and smiled. The young princess gazed at it in wonder and delight. She was smitten to the heart by its beauty and helplessness, and was filled with compassion. Glancing covertly about her, she said to her handmaid: "See now, this must be one of the Hebrew women's children. What shall be done to keep it safe—for surely it is in great danger?"

At this, the child's sister, who had been intently watching all that took place, drew near, and bowing herself before the daughter of Pharaoh, asked if she should go and call one of the Hebrew women, to nurse and tend it.

"Do as thou sayest," said the daughter of Pharaoh, "and go quickly, for I know not how long the child has been without food."

Her heart bounding with joy and excitement, the little maid at once ran off to her mother and told her everything that she had seen and heard. They came back together, and the daughter of Pharaoh, after but one look into the woman's face, gave the babe into her keeping.

"Take this child into thy charge," she said, "nurse it most carefully, and see that no harm come to it. If any should ask whose child it is, send word at once to me, and I will protect thee. It shall stay with thee until it is grown a little, and is of an age to be safe with me. And thou shalt have the wages due to thee."

At this the woman—who was indeed the child's own mother—could hardly keep back her tears, for joy. She bowed herself before the daughter of Pharaoh and in all things did as she was bidden. From that day on her care was over. She loved the child ever more dearly, her one sorrow being the thought that he would some day be taken away from her. And the daughter of Pharaoh provided all that was needful for the well-being and comfort of mother and son.

As soon as he was grown to be of an age when he no longer needed her, his mother brought him to the daughter of Pharaoh. She rejoiced to see this lovely child. Slaves were appointed whose only duty it was to wait upon him and to bring him up as if he were by birth and right of the royal house. The princess treated him in all things as if he were her own son, and she called him Moses, which means "Child of the Waters". For—as if some compassionate divinity had hidden him there—had she not found him among the reeds and rushes by the river's brink?

The Burning Bush

As Moses grew up, he revealed rare gifts of mind and spirit. He was by nature quiet and patient and not easily roused. But, once angered, his heart burned like a furnace, and when he was resolved on a thing no earthly power could turn him aside from it. His dark eyes were set deep beneath clear-cut brows and, unlike the young men of the Egyptians, a short square beard covered his cheek and chin.

What he gave his mind to he mastered; and though he was slow of speech, he was of a spirit that could persist, and press on through all dangers and hindrances. He was a born leader of men and of a will that commands armies. He became learned in all the wisdom of the Egyptians, and while still in his youth was admitted to the college of the priests in On or Heliopolis, the City of the Sun, where the father of Joseph's wife had been High Priest. There, as legend tells, he was known as Asrasif.

But though he was of the high-born company of the priests, he kept himself apart from their mysteries and rites in the vast and solemn temple of Osiris, mightiest of the divinities worshipped by the ancient Egyptians, and judge of the the under-world of their dead. Like Joseph before him, he was faithful to the Lord God of Israel. He prayed to him in solitude under the open heavens, his face towards the east.

Obedient none the less to the severe discipline of the priests, he shared with them in all exercises of the mind—music and geometry and mathematics, and was familiar with the secret knowledge and magic of his own age, and the lore of the starry-minded Chaldeans, the Assyrians, and the Greeks.

He was skilled, too, it is recorded, in the knowledge and strategy of war, and served as an officer in the armies of Egypt when they defeated the invading hordes of the Ethiopians. From childhood he had been accustomed to the graces and manners and luxury of an Egyptian palace, but he knew of what race he was, and that he owed his life and all that he had to his mother's love, and his heart grieved continually over the tribulations of Israel.

When Moses was grown up and in the full years of his manhood, he set out one day, as was his custom, to visit his own people. And he came to where slave-gangs of the Hebrews were at work under their foremen and an Egyptian overseer. By means of wooden rollers laid upon the sand, they were hauling a prodigious stone that had been hewn out of its quarry to the place where it was to be used for building.

The sun blazed down upon the tawny sands of the desert; the air shimmered like molten glass. These Hebrews, haggard and emaciated, stared like brute beasts; the hands of those as yet not broken in to the rope were blistered and bleeding. And as Moses watched them, they stayed a moment to recover their breath, panting with exhaustion, the sweat streaming down from their shaven heads and sun-scorched faces.

But the master of the slave-gang gave them no respite. With curses and lashes he drove them on, treating them with less forbearance than he would even things without life. In pity of their misery Moses could hardly restrain the rage and grief that flamed up in him. He turned swiftly away and strode on.

Throughout the day their cowed and hopeless faces, the looks they had cast him, their weal-scarred shoulders, haunted his mind. He poured out his indignation to his elder brother, Aaron, sharing with him his shame and sorrow at the woes of Israel.

Still in this trouble of soul, he was returning alone a little before nightfall by the way he had come, when a cry of anguish suddenly pierced the quiet, so shrill and piteous that it might be that of a snared beast in the throes of death. He turned aside instantly out of the track. It was no beast that had uttered the cry, but a young Hebrew, one of his own kindred, who was pleading in vain for mercy against the cruelties of an Egyptian that stood over him.

Unseen of either, Moses drew swiftly near. He glanced hither and thither; there was no man in sight. And like an angel of wrath he ran in upon the Egyptian, smote him, and flung him lifeless to the ground. All sounds were hushed in the evening peace. He was alone, trembling and shivering, and cold with dread. He stooped and looked: and stared on in horror of what he had done. At length he hastily scooped out a hole with his hands and hid the body of the Egyptian in the sand.

All that night he lay without sleep and could get no release from the torment of his thoughts. The scene of his wild act of vengeance hung like a picture in the vacancy of the dark, and he was stricken with remorse.

He rose early and went out secretly to the place where he had hidden the body of the Egyptian. And as he drew near in the red glow of the morning, he saw two Hebrews who were bitterly quarrelling. Before he could come to them, one struck the other down with the staff he carried. His face was distorted with rage and hatred. Moses ran in and raised the fallen man from the ground, and staunched his wound.

"Why dost thou strike this man?" he reproached the other. "What evil has he done? Is he not of our blood, mine and thine? Surely we at least should be at one together, and not add to the miseries of Israel?"

The man turned and cursed him. "Who art thou to come meddling and spying?" he cried. "Who appointed thee a priest and judge over us? Wouldst thou murder me as thou didst yesterday murder the Egyptian? Beware of it!"

His voice rang out loud and clear in the bright air. Moses turned swiftly and hastened away, sick to the soul, and helpless. What he had thought to be a secret had been revealed. Only a sprinkling of sand covered the body of the Egyptian from the sight of man. He feared the vengeance of Pharaoh; his one hope of safety was to flee out of the country while yet there was time.

When indeed this matter was reported to the king, he was filled with wrath. He had no love for Moses, who was of the blood of the Hebrews, not Egyptian, though he had proved his skill and resource in war. The king saw in him a danger, and already suspected him of treason. And now that he had occasion, he sought how he might kill him. But it was too late. He had already escaped beyond the fortresses on the frontiers of Egypt, nor did he pause in his flight until he found himself in a region south of the land of Midian and eastward of the Red Sea. There in ancient times were the turquoise and copper mines of the kings of Egypt.

After long wandering Moses came at evening, when the sun was low, to a well, where there was a grove of acacia trees. Wearied out in mind and body, but at last out of danger of pursuit, he sat down to rest. The shade was cool

[145]

after the heat of the day, the earth lay at peace beneath the flaming skies of sunset, and a slender crescent moon was in the west.

Now the priest of the Midianites who dwelt near there had seven daughters. And a little while after Moses had come to the well-side, these seven came down with their father's flocks, and began to fill with water the stone troughs that lay beside it, to water their sheep. And as they did so in the wild bright light of the desert skies, they talked merrily together, their sheep and lambs bleating thirstily around them.

They had been there but a little while, however, when fierce and morose herdsmen of the desert also came down with their flocks, and drove their sheep away. Moses at once rose up and defended them against the shepherds, and himself watered the sheep. The damsels thanked him, marvelling who this stranger could be.

When they returned home to their father, Jethro, he asked them, "How is it you are come back so early this evening?"

They told him of all that had happened at the well, and how a stranger, an Egyptian, had not only protected them from the shepherds, but had helped them to draw water and to give drink to their sheep.

"But where is this Egyptian?" said their father. "Why have you let him go? Haste, now, and bring him in, that I myself may thank him and that he may eat with us." They went out gladly and brought Moses in.

Moses supped with them that evening, and talked with Jethro late, and slept in his house. The days went by, and still he stayed on as Jethro's guest. The seven daughters of the priest never wearied of listening as he talked with their father of the wonders of Egypt, its prodigious funeral pyramids reared up by kings of bygone dynasties in the sands of the desert, the solemn temples to its gods, its lore and magic and learning, and the splendours of the City of the Sun. He spoke of the Pharaoh, too, that now sat upon the throne, and of his victories and conquests. And their hearts melted with pity as he recounted the woes of his fellow-country-men.

At length Jethro persuaded his guest to go no further, but remain with them and become one of his household. Moses was well-content to do so, though at times he was sick for home and pined to return to his own land and to his own people. But he knew that the vengeance of Pharaoh against any who had angered and defied him never faltered or slept, and that to go back was to die.

And Jethro gave Moses his daughter Zipporah in marri-age. Two sons were born to him. To his first-born Moses gave the name of Gershom, which means a Stranger, for he himself was a sojourner in a strange land. The other he named Eliezer, which means the Help of God, for in the day of his need God had delivered him from the vengeance of Pharaoh.

The years that Moses spent in the household of his father-in-law in the country of the Midianites—a people who in time to come were to be one of the fiercest enemies of Israel —were serene and happy. He was never to see their like again.

Now in the process of time the king of Egypt died, and his embalmed body with all pomp and ceremony was laid to rest in the innermost chamber of the secret tomb which he had himself caused to be hewn out of the rock in the desolate valley of the dead. And his son reigned in his stead.

This Pharaoh, who was advanced in age when he came to

the throne, had neither the courage nor the sagacity of his father. He was treacherous and boastful, stubborn and crafty. The Hebrews soon had cause to hate and fear him, for he was as pitiless as he was weak. They groaned under burdens too heavy to be borne, and their cry went up to God to deliver them.

And God heard their cries. He remembered the covenant and bond of peace that he had made with Abraham and Isaac and Jacob, and he took compassion upon them. And though they knew it not, the long years of their affliction in Egypt were nearly at an end.

At the approach of summer, when the rains were over and gone, and the sun burned hot in the sky, the grass-land in the region of Midian where lived Jethro the priest began to dry up and wither. And, as was usual at this season, Moses, who had charge of Jethro's flock, led his sheep far back across the wilderness to the lower uplands of the sacred mountain called Horeb, or Sinai. It was a region of vast steeps of naked rock, an inhuman silent solitude; its crags bleached with sun and tempest, its stones burnished by sharp winds and drifts of sand. Few living creatures roved in the gaunt shadow of these prodigious peaks of granite, only the wild goat found a footing there. And flights of birds could be seen on high winging across to Arabia. But Moses had always found happiness and peace in solitude. His own thoughts and reveries sufficed for company at need. Here, the thin mountain turf was green and sweet; and he stayed for many days in these desolate uplands, stark and affrighting even to those whose home was the wilderness; his dogs and sheep his only companionship.

The silence around him stilled mind and heart. Yet he longed for news of those he loved and from whom he had been separated so many years. The wrongs of Israel had never throughout these years of exile ceased to grieve and trouble him.

One morning early before the dews had dried, he led his flock to fresh pastures, and there he lay down to rest, his staff in his hand, his dogs around him, while his sheep and lambs, each with its own gentle shadow beside it on the sward, grazed peacefully on. And as he sat alone, he fell into a reverie, and his spirit wandered far. Dwindling in distance, the eagle-haunted crags and crests of the mountains towered into the blue waste of noon, while near at hand rose sheer the steeps of Horeb, its summit hidden in cloud. The scream of a bird rang in his ear, and aroused him from his reverie.

And lo, lifting up his eyes, he saw, above and beyond the rock-strewn slope of the valley that mounted up before him, and in a place bare and treeless, a burning bush. The flame of its burning went up from it as from a torch, clear and fervent in the noon-day sun. But though the bush burned on as if with fire, it was not consumed. For the flame was not of earth, but was the glory of an angel of the lord.

Moses gazed at it in wonder, and at length arose, saying within himself: "What marvel is this? I will turn aside and draw near and see this strange sight, why the bush is not burnt."

Leaving his flocks to roam as they willed, he went on up the valley into the solitude of the mountain.

When the Angel of the Lord saw that Moses had turned aside and drew near, he called to him from out of the midst of the burning bush, "Moses, Moses!"

There was no sound else between earth and heaven, and Moses stayed where he stood, his eyes fixed on its miraculous radiance. So still and clear was the voice that it might have called to him from out of the inmost silence of his mind. And he answered the angel: "Here am I."

Then said the angel of the Lord: "Come not hither; but put off thy sandals from off thy feet, for the place whereon thou standest is holy ground. I speak to thee in the name of the Lord God who sent me hither, the God thy father worshipped, yea, the God of Abraham, the God of Isaac, the God of Jacob."

And Moses hid his face, for he was afraid to look upon God. And the voice said: "I have seen the affliction of my people in Egypt and I have heard their wailing by reason of the taskmasters that oppress them. I know their sorrows; and am come down to deliver them and to send thee thyself to Pharaoh the King that thou mayest set my people free and lead them out of Egypt."

The words rang sweet as a clarion in Moses' ears, yet his heart misgave him. "Alas, Lord," he said, "who am I—an outcast and a fugitive condemned to death—that I should confront Pharaoh face to face and bring forth the people of Israel from out of Egypt."

The Lord said: "Be not afraid; I will surely be with thee. All those who sought to kill thee in Egypt are now dead. And for token that it is I, the Lord, who am sending thee thither, the day shall come when thou thyself and all Israel shall serve and worship me upon this sacred mountain."

Moses, still communing with himself, turned his face away and gazed out over the valley where his sheep were placidly browsing and into the distance towards Egypt. And the light of the flame of the burning bush smote on his face, gilding it as if with gold, and the whole earth was still as though in trance.

"But it may be", he said, "when I come before the people and tell them, 'The God of Israel hath sent me, and I come to do his will,' that they will challenge me, and say: 'But who is this God of whom thou speakest: and what is his name?' How then shall I answer them?"

And the Lord God, speaking through the mouth of the angel, answered Moses and said: "I AM THAT I AM: eternal, infinite, the source of all life, all love, all wisdom. And to thee and to my people I will be all that I will reveal myself to be, though as yet thou hast no knowledge of it. Assemble the elders of Israel and proclaim to them: 'Jehovah, the Lord God of your fathers, who was, and is, and ever shall be, hath sent me unto you. I AM hath sent me unto you'. This is my name and it shall be my memorial to all generations. Then say this unto them: 'The Lord God of Israel knows all your sorrows and has seen your distress, and he himself will lead you out and set you free from your bondage in Egypt and bring you up at length into the land that he promised to Abraham, to Isaac and to Jacob, even into Canaan, a good and fruitful land, a land flowing with milk and honey.' And they will listen and pay heed to thee. Then thou and the elders of Israel shall come together into the presence of Pharaoh the king of Egypt, and thou shalt say to him: 'The Lord God of the Hebrews hath revealed himself to us and called us to do his bidding. We entreat thee to let us go three days' journey out of Egypt into the solitude of the wilderness that we may make solemn sacrifice to the Lord our God.'

"But the King of Egypt will refuse to hearken. He is arrogant and stubborn, and no plea or entreaty will move him or cause him to waver. Then shall I stretch forth my hand and I shall smite Egypt with my marvels. Egypt shall be afflicted and all men shall wonder. In that day not only shall this Pharaoh set my people free, but they shall go rejoicing, with their sons and their daughters, and burdened with the riches of Egypt, jewels of silver and jewels of gold, and fine raiment. The proud and haughty of Egypt shall heap gifts upon them and shall urge them to hasten and be gone."

But Moses, still doubting within himself, answered and said: "But even yet it may be that when I appear before the elders of Israel and say the Eternal hath sent me, and declare the sacred name, they may still refuse to believe me, and deny that I come from God. How then shall I give proof of it?"

The voice said: "What is it in thy hand?"

He answered: "My shepherd's staff."

Then said the Lord: "Cast it upon the ground."

Moses, as he was bidden, flung down his staff, and behold, as it touched the rock on which it fell, it became a serpent, living and venomous, and Moses started back from it in fear.

Then said the Lord: "Put out thy hand without fear and seize the serpent by the tail."

Moses stooped, and seized the serpent; and its being changed, and lo, it was his shepherd's staff that was again in his hand.

Then said the Lord: "Thrust thy hand into thy bosom."

He did so. And when he plucked it out of his bosom, it had become like the silvery hand of a leper and was white as snow.

Then said the voice: "Cover thy hand again."

And when Moses withdrew his hand, it no longer resembled that of a leper, but was restored to the likeness of the other.

Then said the Lord: "If when thou appear before the elders of Israel, they believe not that thou art come from the Eternal, and refuse to be convinced either by the one sign I have given thee or by the other, and will not listen to thee, then do thou fill a vessel with the water of the river of Egypt and pour it out upon the parched sands on the bank of the river, and the water which thou hast taken out of the river shall become red as blood upon the sand."

Then said Moses: "O Lord God, I beseech thee to have patience with me. I am by nature slow and halting of speech and ever have been. Nor even while thou hast been speaking with me have I been able to say what is in my heart, for I am a man without any skill in the use of words. How then shall I speak before the elders of Israel so that they shall be persuaded and believe in me, and that thou hast sent me?"

And God said to Moses: "Who made the mouth of man? Who causes this man to be dumb and that deaf, and who gives or withholds the sight of man's eyes? Is it not the Lord God, the creator of all? Go then, and think no more how thou shalt say what I have bidden thee say, for I myself will guide thy tongue and give thee speech."

Moses bowed his head in deep and perplexed thought. He was divided in mind. All his heart's longing was to obey the will of the Lord for the redemption of his people. Yet distrust of himself and of his own powers still held him back. His voice trembled. "So be it, O Lord," he said. "And yet I would that the Lord would send someone to speak for him better able than I am!"

At this, the anger of the angel of the Lord was kindled against Moses. "Hast thou forgotten Aaron thy brother?" he said. "Is he not a Levite and a priest, and hath he no gift of words? Even now he is on his way hither to meet thee, and when he seeth thee, his heart will be filled with joy. Do thou then speak with him, and inspire and direct him in all that he shall say. Thou shalt tell him of the wonders that have been shown to thee this day. I have made thee my prophet before Israel and before the King of Egypt, and Aaron thy brother shall be thy spokesman. In all things thou shalt be his inspiration, as if thou thyself wert of God, and he thy prophet. Take thy staff, and this rod that I give into thy hand. With it thou shalt do miracles and show that I the Eternal am with thee."

The voice ceased and Moses was alone. High overhead the virgin crest of Horeb pierced the sky, its shadow flung dark across the hollow steep on which he stood, as the sun went down into the west. The flame, pure as crystal and of the light of gold, that had dwelt in the midst of the bush yet had touched neither twig nor leaf with fire, no longer shone upon his face and filled his mind with its radiance, for the angel of the Lord had gone his way.

The Petition to Pharaoh

Moses went down into the valley and gathered together his flock and led them back across the desert to Jethro. He said nothing of what had passed during the days of his absence. His face was changed. The vision he had seen haunted his eyes. He spoke like one who has been very near to death and what lies beyond it, and whose mind is far away. He told Jethro that he wished to leave his service awhile, and to return into Egypt. "Let me go, I pray thee," he said, "so that I may visit my own people again and those near and dear to me in my own country, for I know not even if they are still alive."

Jethro was very gracious to him; the years they had spent together had deepened their affection one for another. He could see that some strange event of which he himself had no knowledge had deeply moved and troubled Moses, and he divined a little of what was in his mind. He asked no questions, but fondly embraced him. "Go in peace," he said, "and may all things be well with thee and with thy brethren from whom thou hast been parted so long."

When they had first met together, Moses had been a stranger, friendless and solitary, his very life in danger. The day was soon to come when he would return into Midian and to Mount Horeb, and they would meet again; but he himself would then no longer be a shepherd of sheep, but the leader and commander of the whole host of Israel.

Having bidden his wife and his two sons farewell, Moses set out on his journey. And while he was passing through the wilderness at the foot of Mount Horeb he met his brother Aaron who was himself come to visit him. He kissed him and great was their happiness. They had much to tell one another; and as they slowly paced along side by side through the parched flats and sandhills of the desert towards Goshen, or sat at evening in the camping-place where they were to sleep, Moses shared with his brother the anxious thoughts that filled his mind. He told him of the wonder of the burning bush and all that the Lord had bidden him do in Egypt, and of the signs and portents that were to be revealed. And they faced together the supreme ordeal that lay before them, giving one another confidence and resolution.

When they came into Goshen, they called together the elders or chief men of Israel, and Aaron revealed to them everything that Moses had told him concerning his communion with the Lord on the sacred mountain of Horeb, and Moses himself showed them the signs and wonders of the Lord. The people believed. The Lord God had seen their sorrow and was compassionate. Their hearts were filled with joy and longing and ardour; they bowed their heads and worshipped.

On a day appointed by Pharaoh, Moses and Aaron and the elders of Israel were brought into the hall of audience in the palace of the king to present their petition. They prostrated themselves before him and made obeisance. And Pharaoh demanded what reason they had for appearing before him.

They answered him: "We come not as suppliants before Pharaoh, but have been sent hither by the Lord, the God of Israel. Our words are his words, and it is his command that we bring to the king. Thus saith the Lord: 'Let my people go out of Egypt that they may make a pilgrimage into the wilderness, and there keep a solemn feast and offer sacrifice to their God'."

As he listened, the face of Pharaoh darkened with scorn and derision. "And who is this God," he said, "that I should regard him? I neither know nor heed him. Nor will I let the Hebrews go."

They answered him: "We entreat thee to have patience and to listen to our petition, seeing that it is not merely we, thy servants, who plead before thee, but the Lord God of the Hebrews who hath made known his will unto us. It is little that we ask: only that our people may be granted a brief respite from their toil in the king's quarries and brick-fields, and may go forth on a three days' pilgrimage into the wilderness, there to sacrifice to their God. Else peradventure some great evil may befall them—pestilence or the sword."

"I say unto thee," said Pharaoh in his wrath, "I neither know this God nor heed him. If God he be, what sign or token canst thou show that he has sent thee? The Gods are mighty, and manifest themselves on earth in marvels beyond man's understanding. You say you are this God's envoys. Give proof of it then, and it may be that Pharaoh himself will do him honour!"

Then in the presence of the king and of his lords and counsellors who were in attendance upon him, Aaron cast down before the throne the rod that was in his hand. And behold, before the eyes of all assembled there, the rod was changed and became a living serpent. They recoiled from it in astonishment and fear. And Aaron stooped and plucked it up from the ground, and it returned to its former shape and semblance, and his rod was again in his hand.

But Pharaoh himself sat unmoved on his throne, a smile

of secret mockery on his high narrow countenance. He
gave command that his wizards or magicians should be
summoned into his presence—men skilled in occult and
secret arts. In the robes of their rites, and each with his
magic wand or rod in his hand, Jannes and Mambres their
leaders, they entered the great hall and made obeisance to
the king. And as Aaron had done, so did they.

They cried their incantations, and cast down their rods
before the throne, and these too of the secret sorcery they
knew became as living serpents. And though Aaron's rod
had the mastery over theirs and swallowed them up, no sign

of wonder or apprehension showed on Pharaoh's face. He turned abruptly and addressed Moses and Aaron by name.

"Now indeed," said he, "can Pharaoh testify how mighty a God has sent you hither! Wondrous in truth are the marvels that he shares with the least of Pharaoh's magicians! But I have heard of you; and nothing good. What insensate folly was this in your minds by which you designed to deceive me? You crave audience of me and avow that some God of the Hebrews—who swarm like pestilent flies in the land—has bidden you go and make merry with him in the wilderness. But what, in the hidden treason of your designs, you are bent on doing is to breed discontent among my work-people, to decoy them away from their labours and pamper them with idleness. Understand then; the Hebrews shall not go; and I warn you to bring no more complaints before me. Look well to it."

That same day Pharaoh sent for the overseers whom he had set over the Hebrews, and commanded that in future not only should the straw that had hitherto been given to them for the making of bricks be withheld, and that the slave-gangs themselves should find where they could what they needed, but that in spite of this the daily tale of bricks required of them should in no degree be reduced.

The overseers and gang-masters made known to the Hebrews that from that day forward, by the king's decree, no more straw would be supplied to them as heretofore out of the royal granaries: and that in future they must find what straw they needed as best they could.

Now the only substitute available was the stubble that had been left in the fields after the gathering in of the harvest. Of long straw they could get none. Then day by day they wearied themselves in the idle and waste labour of grubbing up this stubble-straw; and the tale of bricks, which each gang was compelled to make, fell short of what was required of them.

And as day by day the overseers and their clerks, on checking the brick-piles, found the quantity of new-made bricks to be far less than was customary, they sent for the Hebrew foremen of the slave-gangs and beat them, threatening that a worse punishment was in store for them if the tale of bricks should fall short on the morrow. Enraged by this injustice, the Hebrew foremen met together and in a mob made their way into the city to appeal to Pharaoh. Herded together in the stifling heat by the armed guards who had been sent out to meet them, they were admitted no further than into the outer precincts of the palace, while two of them were led in before the king.

"We come to Pharaoh", they said, "to plead for justice. Why are his servants so vilely treated? The overseers goad us on and rage against us: 'Make brick, make brick!' But how shall bricks be made without straw? And why are we pitilessly beaten if a full day's tale of bricks fall short of what it should when half thy servants' time from dawn till dark must be spent in scrabbling stubble out of the fields? The blame is not ours but Pharaoh's and his overseers', who deal unjustly with his servants."

Then said Pharaoh: "Return thanks to what gods you have if, ere night come, you hang not by the neck to the loftiest gallows in Egypt. It is not because you have too much but too little to do that you come flocking out of Goshen in a rebellious rabble to make complaint. You are idle: you are idle! This also is why I am pestered with men of your race, puffed up with pride and folly, and asserting that some God requires your sacrifices in the sands of the desert. Begone from out of the city and trouble Pharaoh no more, lest the full vengeance of his wrath fall upon you, and that soon!"

And he decreed that the daily labour of the Hebrews should not be reduced by a single brick. The foremen of the slave-gangs were driven like sheep to the slaughter from out of the city. Their appeal to Pharaoh had left them in worse straits than before. They were indeed in evil case; on the one side an implacable tyrant and his overseers; and on the other the resentment of the Israelites who, worn-out with this double toil, worked under them and for whom they were answerable.

As they went on their way, disputing together and racked with the rough usage they had received, they encountered Moses and Aaron. Eager for news of what had passed, they had come out to meet them. The mob raged with fury at sight of them.

"Be God our witness of the evil you have brought on us," they shouted against them, "and may he judge between us and reward you as you deserve! You have poisoned the mind of Pharaoh against us, and made us to stink in the nostrils of all Egypt. And now because of your meddlings he will not rest until he has destroyed us altogether."

Moses turned away and left them, their menaces and reproaches ringing in his ears. As soon as he was alone, in anguish of soul he poured out all that was in his heart to the Lord. All that he had attempted had come to nothing. Pharaoh had not only contemptuously rejected his petition, but had avenged himself on the Israelites and embittered them against himself.

"O Lord God," he cried in his misery, "why hast thou chosen me, and yet hast forsaken me? All that I do is in vain."

And as he prayed, his mind became more serene. And the

Lord comforted Moses in the solitude of his communion with him.

"I am Jehovah the Lord God," he said, "who appeared unto Abraham and Isaac and Jacob; I am the Almighty whom they themselves worshipped. But they knew me only in part and could conceive of me only as their own hearts revealed to them. They knew not that I am the Eternal, who was and is and ever shall be. Yet it was I the Lord who established my covenant with them, that I would give the land of Canaan—the land wherein they themselves sojourned—to their children's children. Speak again to my people. Bid them have faith and be not cast down. The Eternal will be their salvation, and will redeem them from all their grief and woe.

"But if heartsick and impatient and made desperate by the cruelties they endure, they reject thee, and refuse to listen to thee, then do thou thyself return again to Pharaoh, and in all things as I bid thee, do. Stubborn with pride is the heart of Pharaoh, and his eyes are darkened. But my wonders shall be revealed, and a day shall come when thou thyself shalt be as a god to him, and he will humble himself before thee and plead with thee to intercede with the Lord of Hosts on his behalf, lest he himself be destroyed."

The Plagues of Egypt

At the season of the annual inundation, when the
waters of the Nile sweep down in flood from the
mountains of Abyssinia, Pharaoh, attended by his
courtiers, his priests and officers, proceeded in
state from his palace to take part in a festival which, as in
years gone by, was to be held upon the river. On his progress thither through the throngs which had come forth to
acclaim him, and before he had embarked into the silken-
sailed vessel that had been prepared for the ceremony and
was moored beside the quay, Moses and Aaron confronted
the king by the riverside, and yet again entreated him to
grant the petition they had made on behalf of the Israelites.
And again he refused to listen to them.

Then in sight of Pharaoh and of the great company assembled there, Moses lifted up his rod and smote the swirling waters. And behold, even as they watched, from shore
to shore the whole surface of the flooding river began to run
red as blood.

But though many were dismayed at this marvel, it moved
Pharaoh not one whit. This also was within the knowledge
of his wizards and magicians, and he paid no heed to it.
When the ceremony was over, he returned to his palace.
Nor did he show any sign of relenting when report was
made to him that a wonder unknown in living memory had
brought horror on the whole city.

For now the river not only continued to flow blood-red,
but the fish in it perished. Its tide was laden with their
puffed-up carcases, floating, belly upwards, as the flood-
water swept from the mountains down to the sea. The river
stank; and not the river alone. The water of the canals also
that had been cut out for the irrigation of the fields glistened
in the light of sunset, red as blood. Even in the reservoirs of
the Egyptians, in their tanks and cisterns, in the very pots
and jars they used in their houses—there was water red as
blood. As it staled it putrefied and became foul and corrupt.
Neither man nor beast dared taste of it. And the Egyptians

were compelled to dig round about the river for water fit to drink, and to sink wells.

So it continued for seven days. And when the seven days were at an end Moses came again into the presence of Pharaoh. He warned him that unless he consented to do as the Lord God of Israel had ordained, the creeping things of the earth would bear witness against him and be a cause of shuddering and dread to the whole realm of Egypt. But Pharaoh stubbornly refused to pay heed to him, and dismissed him with contempt.

And even as Moses had foretold, there began to breed in the corrupt and blood-red waters of the river an unprecedented plague of frogs. The mud-shallows amidst the beds of reeds and rushes and the fringes of the water were soon astir and alive with them. They crawled up in an innumerable host from out of the swamps. They spread in myriads over the low-lying lands on either bank of the river, and swarmed everywhere, creeping and hopping not only into the orchards and gardens, fresh and lovely with their leafy trees and flowers, and into the lilied pools and conduits, but into the innermost rooms of the houses of the Egyptians, their bedchambers and their beds, their cooking stoves or ovens, and even into the bowls in which they kneaded their dough for the making of bread. Squat and noisome, there was no cranny or crevice free from them.

Clammy and cold as the mire from which they came, they climbed up, in the dead of night, upon the Egyptians' bodies as they lay asleep, and leapt about the clods in myriads as they worked in the fields. The air resounded with their croaking. Swarms of these harmless, bright-coloured creatures had been seen in Egypt in previous years, to be soon devoured by the waterfowl or to return into the Nile. But there is horror to man in nature's multitudes, and now, leaping and creeping, or staring and inert, they swarmed in every dwelling, even in the houses of the wealthiest nobles and the private chambers of Pharaoh and his queen.

The Egyptians were filled with loathing of the frogs. Why had their gods brought such a visitation upon them? If magic could bring such a pest, why could it not be conjured away? But the priests and sorcerers could do nothing. At length Pharaoh himself sent for the chiefs of the Hebrews and commanded Moses to intercede with his God.

"Think not", he said, "it is beyond the power and knowledge of my magicians to breed frogs. That is simple of proof. But to rid Egypt swiftly, and as with a gesture, of the plague of them that now afflicts the land—that were in truth a wonder. Entreat thy God, then, to remove this vexation from the land, seeing that it is a cause of distress to my people and an affront even to me myself. Then shall I know that he is indeed a mighty God, and that it is fitting the Hebrews should be given grace from their labour in order that they may do him honour."

Moses stayed a moment before he made answer to the king.

"What is thy servant", he said at last, "compared with Pharaoh, lord of all! Thou thyself shalt have this glory over me, and shalt decide at what hour I am to entreat the God of the Hebrews on thy behalf."

Pharaoh gazed at him stonily but concealed his anger. "Why, then, let it be to-morrow, and ere the sun set," he answered. And this he said to try Moses, for he had no belief in his mind that the plague was other than a visitation of nature.

Then said Moses: "So be it. To-morrow I will make my prayer, and the frogs shall be destroyed, and from that day onward none shall be found alive anywhere in Egypt, except only in the waters of the river. By this shalt thou know that there is in power none like unto the Lord our God; and that when he commands, the mightiest must obey."

The plague of frogs ceased. They perished suddenly in their myriads in the fields and orchards, in the gardens and the houses, and wheresoever they had crept for harbourage. Alive they had been pest enough, dead they were a foulness. The Egyptians, to be rid of their carcases, raked them together and piled them up in heaps that rotted in the sun. The air was filled with their stench.

But when it was reported to Pharaoh that as if by a marvel the land had been suddenly freed of this plague, and that to him had been accorded the renown of it, his mood changed. As lightly as he had given his word, so he dismissed all thought of it from his mind.

And Moses stretched out his hand, and with his rod he smote the dust of Egypt, as he had smitten the flooding waters of the Nile. And lo, in the brooding heat of the sun, from the sod-caked shallows of the river there issued a venomous swarm of gnats. They rose, droning, like clouds of fine dust into the air, their wings shimmering glass-like, the sound of them faint and shrill as a harp-string. Athirst for blood, they pestered man and beast both day and night, so that none could get peace or rest from them.

When Pharaoh summoned his wizards and bade them with their magic incantations breed life out of the dust, though in fear of his vengeance they made no answer at that time, they knew that all their enchantments would be in vain. This wonder was beyond their magic, and they themselves were dismayed and gave Pharaoh warning. "We entreat Pharaoh to beware," they said. "These vile Hebrews have knowledge to bring about mysteries of which we ourselves are ignorant. What now is all about us, haunting the

very air we breathe, is no magic, but a cause of grave disquiet. We see in it the finger of God."

Yet such was Pharaoh's pride and self-will that he refused to listen to their counsel. In his vengeful malice
against the Hebrews his heart was hardened, and the dews
of the mercy of heaven were withdrawn from him because
of his stubborn opposition to the will of God that he knew
and feared yet refused to obey. He denied further audience
to the Hebrews. And when Moses intercepted and confronted him as in his two-horsed chariot he proceeded with
his courtiers on his way to the river, and warned him that
unless he relented, worse evils would assuredly follow, he in-
voked the curses of his gods upon him and, his countenance
distorted with rage, drove furiously on.

But repentance followed hard upon his folly. The wind
veered, and began to blow softly yet persistently from out
of the south—parching and sultry. And borne in on the
stream of it there flitted in upon Egypt legions of dog-flies.
Hovering in the air or crawling upon the ground, they
crept into every byre and stable and pen and dwelling-
house, and were a torment and a curse to all within their
walls. The children wailed for pain and weariness. Man's
business was brought almost to a standstill. Nor does the
dog-fly betray its onset with the twangling of its wings. It
settles in silence, stabs with its sharp weapon into the living
flesh, and the pang of it is a warning that comes too late.

Yet though throughout the length and breadth of Egypt
there was no escape from this blood-sucking pest of dog-
flies, the land of Goshen where dwelt the people of Israel
was wholly free from them. The Hebrews groaned under
persecutors as pitiless in human shape, but of dog-flies there
was none.

The ravages of these flies among the Egyptians became

at last beyond endurance, and Pharaoh sent in haste into Goshen for Moses and Aaron. They made obeisance to him where he sate in splendour in the midst of his court upon the royal dais, under its canopy of gold and blue and scarlet. But he was compelled to raise his voice to make himself audible above the droning of the dog-flies. He spoke harshly, his face enflamed, his voice hoarse with rage and chagrin.

"Up, and delay not, but get you gone," he said. "Your petition is granted. Return at once from whence you came. Prepare to make your feast in Goshen and there sacrifice to your God. Three days' grace, and three days' grace only, shall be given you, and my overseers and taskmasters shall be withdrawn meanwhile."

He appeared to speak in haste and as if without forethought, yet his words were as crafty as his intention. And Moses was not deceived.

"Our petition to the king", he made answer, "was that he should give grace to the Hebrews to make a three days' pilgrimage into the wilderness, to hold a solemn feast there, and there only, to the one true God. Beasts, then, in plenty we shall need for sacrifice, oxen and bullocks. But as Pharaoh knows well, these are held sacred to their gods by the Egyptians, and it would be a needless cause of offence to them if we remain in Goshen and sacrifice there. There would be riot and tumult. The people would rise up and stone the Hebrews, and bloodshed would follow. Nay, O king, it is into the wilderness that the children of Israel must go, and not less than three days' journey, for such is the will of God."

Pharaoh sat motionless, his lean cheek resting on his hand, his face set in a sullen frown. There was silence in the great hall, but for the whispering stir of the dog-flies.

"So be it," he said at last. "There is wisdom in your appeal to me; and it is true there might be this danger. The least sign of riot or rebellion is hateful to me and would meet with instant retribution. Let then the Hebrews go their way well beyond the confines of Egypt into the desert. But not too far: too far, I say. And now delay no longer, but intercede between me and the Lord thy God."

"Thou hast spoken," said Moses. "I go now to entreat the Lord to free Pharaoh and his people from the visitation that he has brought upon them. But let not Pharaoh vaunt himself over me if the Lord be merciful; and let him not in mockery deceive me yet again, and yet again withdraw the consent that he has now given that my people shall go in peace and sacrifice to their God."

God answered Moses' entreaty, and the dog-flies ceased in Egypt. And yet, once again, Pharaoh the King was false to his own word, hardened his heart, and returned to his obstinacy as of old.

And retribution speedily followed. There came a dreadful murrain or pestilence that spread through Egypt, attacking the cattle, the horses, the oxen, the sheep, and even the camels of the traders that were in the land at that season, so that multitudes of them languished and died of its ravages. Yet of the flocks and herds that belonged to the people of Israel in Goshen none was harmed, and not a single one perished.

Word of this being brought to Pharaoh, he himself made inquiry of his overseers. They reported that the cattle of the Hebrews had wholly escaped the pestilence, that it raged only in Egypt. Nevertheless, he disregarded it. And while the murrain was still in the land, Moses and Aaron went out and met Pharaoh in the way as he was returning into his palace. And when he refused to listen to them, Moses was consumed with anger at this fresh insult to the Lord. He snatched up two handfuls of soot or ashes from out of a kiln, used in the baking of pots and glasswork, that stood near, and before the very eyes of the king tossed them on high and sprinkled them towards heaven.

"Lo, now: watch thou and wait!"

The ashes were scattered; a light wind carried the dust of them hither, thither, and dispersed it far and wide. And behold, there broke out on the bodies of man and beast foul boils and swelling blains, inflaming the skin. Nor did the courtiers and noblemen of Pharaoh's household escape this malady, nor even his priests and magicians.

For when one morning early, after days of weary waiting, Moses once more demanded an audience of the king, not one of the magicians was present. They were disgraced and in deep despondency, and their very faces were so disfigured by reason of the boils upon them, that they were ashamed to show themselves and be humbled before him.

Yet again Moses warned Pharaoh of what would ensue if he continued to ignore and defy the will of God. He foretold that on the morrow there would descend such a storm of hail on Egypt as had never been witnessed since the foundation of the kingdom. Pharaoh himself affected to be unmoved, and answered him disdainfully. But many of his counsellors and officers of state who were present, having taken to heart the wonders that had already been revealed, had come to fear the Hebrews and the God they worshipped. They gave orders secretly to their servants that from daybreak till nightfall on the morrow not one of their herdsmen was to drive his cattle afield. Let him keep them safe in shed, and himself indoors.

Pharaoh slept uneasily that night, fell into a fitful slumber a little before dawn, but awoke again early and rose from his bed to look out from his window at the skies of morning. A scene of splendour and ill-boding met his gaze. Mounting into the vacancy of the heavens and borne upon a wind counter to that which breathed fitfully then died down and rose again on the earth, vast leaden clouds, domed and turreted and utterly dwarfing in their majesty even the temples and palaces of the city, were lit with the silvery radiance of the rising sun.

They towered higher and higher until the whole firmament was concealed, and the light died. And it was as though morning were retreating into the glooms of night. And as Pharaoh watched, out of the hush and stagnancy of the heavens a tempest of wind suddenly swept across the city, and the livid dark was riven by a burst of flame, dazzling his eyes, so that he clapped his hands over them to shut out the glare. For a few moments he stood blinded and motionless, while the very stones of his palace trembled beneath him at the crash of thunder.

And after the thunder came a storm of hail. It whitened instantly as if with hoarfrost the whole valley lying on either side the looping waters of the great river. Throughout the confines of Egypt the steady tumult of its falling could be heard even above the reverberations of the thunder, and the fire of the lightning ran along upon the earth, now hoary with hailstones of ice. The men and the cattle that had escaped the pestilence and that were exposed to this tempest of hail fled in panic for shelter, smitten as they ran by its sharp-edged shards of ice. Within a few minutes from its first onset the crops of ripening barley were utterly ruined, and the blue-flowering flax was beaten to the ground and laid low. The fields of wheat and of spelt that were as yet only in the green blade alone escaped. Never had the like of it been seen before in Egypt.

In the midst of the tempest Pharaoh sent in hot haste for Moses. He sat pale and trembling, his voice scarcely audible in the din of the thunder and the hail, while the lightnings glimmering overhead filled the great chamber with their wild blue light. And he confessed that he had sinned.

"The God of Israel is a God of righteousness," he said. "I and my people are in the wrong. Entreat this God to still these mighty thunderings and to stay this hail. They oppress my very soul. I will let the Hebrews go and you shall stay no longer."

And Moses answered the king: "As soon as I am gone out from the presence of Pharaoh and have departed out of the city, I will lift my hands in supplication to the Lord, and the thunders shall cease in heaven and there shall be no more hail. Thou hast vaunted thyself in thy pride, and he has been merciful. With but one deadly pestilence he might have smitten Egypt and swept away both thee and thy people like chaff before the wind from off the face of the earth. The soul of Pharaoh is in the hands of God. Thou hast been preserved only that thou mayest acknowledge his power and be the cause of his honour and glory throughout the world. But that day is not yet. Thou hast professed to be penitent, but the words of thy mouth are one thing and the heart within thee another. And I know well that in thy secret mind and in the minds of thy priests and counsellors there is no true fear of God."

Moses turned and left him. The hail abated and the lightnings and the thunderings ceased. The sun shone out again in splendour, but on an Egypt ravaged with storm, its fields of harvest sodden and desolate. And when Pharaoh saw that all again seemed well and fair, he flattered himself that by his cunning pretences he had once more outwitted the leaders of the Hebrews. None the less he was shaken in spirit. He not only hated Moses but feared him, and was disquieted with dread of the divine power he still defied but could no longer challenge or refute.

Egypt is Afraid

Days and weeks passed by, yet reports continued to reach the king of the havoc that had been caused by the tempest and the pestilence and by the disasters that had gone before. His realm was seething with discontent. Rumours that Jehovah, the God of the Hebrews, was the cause of their troubles had filled the people with fear and dark forebodings. The whole traffic and commerce of the country was almost at a standstill and its market places were deserted and empty of merchandise. Moreover, report of the fatalities that had fallen upon Egypt had already spread far beyond its confines and among kings and nations ever awaiting an opportunity to assail her when she showed signs of weakness or was divided against herself. In the midst of these cares and anxieties, Moses appeared yet again in the presence of Pharaoh. He was received in one of the lesser rooms of the palace and but a few of the king's most confidential advisers were in attendance upon him.

"Thou hast seen. Thou hast heard," said Moses. "Thou knowest the evils that have come upon Egypt. At the mere nod of thy head my people could go free to worship their God. Yet again, and yet again, hast thou withdrawn the solemn word spoken with thine own mouth. Take warning, O king, while still there is time. Heed now, though it be late, the will of God that I have made known to thee, lest his judgment fall upon thee yet more heavily and thou cry unto him, but in vain, in despair and remorse. For I say unto thee, if still thou art obdurate, after the tempest shall come the locusts. They shall descend upon Egypt and shall devour every green thing growing that has escaped the hail. Their destruction shall be such as none alive has witnessed since the day that he was born!"

When he had withdrawn from the presence of the king, his nobles and counsellors began to murmur among themselves. They had the welfare of Egypt at heart. And though few of them were yet convinced that the calamities which had befallen the country were due to the intervention of a God they neither knew nor reverenced, they had themselves seen the bitter humiliation of Pharaoh's priests and magicians. They had learned also that this detested leader of the Hebrews was a man to whom all their abstruse and secret learning was an open book; that his deed assuredly followed his word; and that he was possessed of powers against which Pharaoh's craft and obstinacy might serve him for a while but which would at last overwhelm him in defeat.

They spoke openly. "How long", they said to Pharaoh, "shall this man be allowed to entice us on from one destruction to another? The whole country has been laid waste by him and is rank with discontent. Pharaoh's enemies exult at news of it. And now this traitor threatens us with yet another plague that will destroy the little that remains to us of our fruit, our crops, our very bread. Famine will surely follow. Our foes will descend on us and the glories and conquests even of the king, thy father, be wiped clean away. These Hebrews ask nothing more than a brief respite from their labours that they may sacrifice to their God. We beseech thee then to placate them and to let them go. The hand of Pharaoh is mighty: he can afford to relax it a little that at his own chosen moment he may clench it the more irresistibly."

But there were others of his counsellors who believed that the appeal made by Moses was merely a device, and that as soon as the Hebrews were released from the discipline and control of their overseers and taskmasters, his design was to lead them in open rebellion against the lordship of Egypt. Pharaoh wavered between the one faction and the other. In spite of what had gone before, he paid little regard to Moses' threat, for locusts were seldom seen in Egypt and seemed to him of small account. But he thought to gain his own ends by compromise and craft. He sent again for Moses and Aaron and those of the elders of Israel who were with them.

"It must by now", said Pharaoh when they were come before him, "have been made plain to you that menaces are powerless to move me. It has never been my desire to refuse whatever may be just and right. In stubborn folly you thought to defy me, and clemency alone has prevented my vengeance from falling not only on you yourselves but on your people. They shall make their pilgrimage; they shall keep their feast in the desert. But first let me know which among them shall be chosen to go, and which of them shall remain in Goshen?"

And Moses answered the king: "We will go with our young and with our old, with our sons and our daughters, with our flocks and our herds. Thus will we go. From greatest to least of us, O King—halt and blind and helpless, the babe at its mother's breast and the old man trembling on the brink of the grave—not one shall remain behind. Israel is one; and the Lord God Jehovah hath bidden Israel to his feast."

Pharaoh turned with a gesture of scorn to the nobles and counsellors who had opposed him. "See now," he cried, "what overweening insolence is this!"

Then he once more confronted Moses. "In sooth," he said, "thy God must be a mighty god if I ever consent to let thy children go. Thine own words have betrayed thee. From first to last thou hast been contriving this secret treason against me, intending when once thy people, these Hebrews, have withdrawn beyond my borders that they shall never return. Mark well: I will have none of it. If you would serve your God, go; but your grown men only; for that and that alone was your petition. I have spoken; trouble me no more!" And he commanded his servants to drive the Hebrews out of his presence.

Then Moses stretched out his rod over the land of Egypt; and a dry and parching wind began to rise from out of the east. It blew, laden with the arid heat of the vast wastes of the wilderness of Arabia and the desert of Syria that is beyond Canaan. And it continued without ceasing all that day and all that night. And behold, on the morrow at daybreak, the locusts came up with the wind.

Drifting in from the sands of the wilderness in which they were engendered, they advanced host upon host, in league-long clouds so dense from their vanguard to their rear that their sun-shimmering wings spread a shade over Egypt and veiled the face of day. The whizzing of their multitudes above the earth awoke even those that slept, and struck terror into all that heard.

Horn and gong sounded the alarm. Men ran this way and that in terror, their beasts in panic. And when about the middle of the morning the wind fell to calm, this living cloud came wafting down like flakes innumerable of drifting snow. Where they settled, there they stayed, their wings close folded, until the earth was mantled in a moving pall and was black with them. They were strown so close where there was any plenty of food that an upper layer of them, eyed and ravenous, straddled over the one beneath; and above that, others. For though the grass-hopper or cricket, which is of the kin of the locusts, is happy company enough to man as he shrills on his blade of grass in the summer sun, or chirps in the warm dark, the ravages of an army of locusts are a loss beyond computation in these countries of the east.

In the stagnant calm that had followed, the murmur of their voracious chirpings and gnawings shook the air. And the locusts devoured every green leaf from off the branches and every sprouting blade of wheat or remnant of barley that the tempest had spared, and the fruit also that was swelling upon the trees. There remained nothing green and verdant on either side the Nile.

Never before in Egypt had there been seen the like of these hosts of locusts for numbers and destruction, and never shall the like be seen again. The people were in despair. They had begun to take heart after the devastation caused by the tempest of hail and lightning; and now the little that had been saved was lost to them for ever. Famine and starvation lay in wait for them; and they saw in this no natural evil but the hand of God. And though in a frenzy of haste they dug deep pits and trenches, and kindled high fires and flame and smoke, the locusts were destroyed in such myriads that their own bodies put out the fires and filled the pits. And still in their multitudes they came marching on. As well hope to repel the flood-tide of the sea.

Hour followed hour of that disastrous day, and messengers from all parts of Egypt were dispatched with urgent reports to Pharaoh from the governors of his provinces and the overseers of his granaries. Even those mounted on horseback were compelled to turn aside to avoid the clotting swarm of locusts that were trampled by thousands under their horses' hoofs. And Pharaoh saw clearly the danger that threatened him if this pest were not speedily removed. He was dismayed; and in his fear he forgot his pride. Without consulting his counsellors and statesmen, he sent urgently for Moses and Aaron, and confessed that he had sinned. He sued them to torgive the affront of which in his haste he had been guilty when at their last audience with him they had been driven by his servants from out of his presence.

"I do entreat thee", he implored Moses, "to mediate between me and the Lord Jehovah yet once again, that he remove this atrocious plague from Egypt. It is unendurable to me. That done, I will decide how what thou askest may best be achieved."

They left him, and he withdrew himself, his mind in torment, and waited for what the day might bring forth. The Lord God heard Moses' prayer. There came a wind from the west, streaming between earth and sky, and the locusts were drawn up in its flood of air and swept like dust from off the floor, and perished in the watery waste of the Red Sea. The fringes of its foam upon the sands of the shore were black with them.

And when Pharaoh was assured that this new danger, like the plagues that had preceded it, was at an end, even yet again his mind and mood abruptly changed. He hardened his heart and returned to his stubborn connivings.

In my own chosen time, he thought within himself, I will consider and will decide this matter. These rebellious Hebrews must be taught that neither they nor their God can compel me to take action against my will. Let them wait until I choose to be gracious. He showed no sign of keeping the solemn protestations he had made to Moses, and did nothing.

Nor did Moses himself as in days gone by appear again before Pharaoh. He too made no sign. He waited in patience —knowing too well this stubborn and feeble king to believe he would keep faith with him.

In due season the will of God was revealed to him. There came a day when he stretched out his rod not over the waters or the dust of Egypt but towards heaven. And at his word the violent and burning wind called Hamsin that springs up from out of the south, from the waste of Libya, began to blow, lifting with its blasts the sand and dust of the desert in billows so dense and lofty that the sun's radiance in mid-heaven, from a brilliant orange, dwindled to a circle red as blood and fainter than that of the moon, and then vanished.

There arose also dense emanations of vapour from out of the ground and the low lands of the river, and all Egypt lay canopied in a hot and unnatural night, in a darkness which may be felt. Finer than crystals of snow the sand borne in on the wind silted through every crevice and cranny and mingled with the Egyptians' victuals, and with their wine and drink. At the distance of a few paces man's shape was blotted out; all sense of direction was lost, so that none dared venture out of doors or stir in the streets. Even within the houses the heated air stifled throat and lungs, and the inmates went groping and stumbling, with nought but their feeble lamps to pierce the gloom. For three days continually they saw not one another, neither rose any from his place to go abroad.

But in the land of Goshen the sun as usual rose and set, and there shone clear the natural light of day.

Towards the close of the third day Pharaoh sent for Moses. After long and fevered debate with his advisers, he was wearied out. Divided in policy, they were at their wits' end; the wiser among them urging him to be rid of the Hebrews for good and all, and to defy the will of God no longer; the rest, obstinate and futile as himself, counselling him to temporize. As was his usual practice, he gave way in a little and trusted to his subtlety.

The lights that had been brought to illumine the great chamber of audience flared dimly in the thick and heated air, scarcely piercing its hollow vault of gloom. And Moses when he was brought into the presence of the king drew nearer to the throne than hitherto. He made obeisance, rose and stood mute. The wafting of the fan-bearers stirred on his cheek. He fixed his eyes through the murk upon Pharaoh's countenance as the king addressed him.

"I have yet again", said Pharaoh, "remembered me the pledge I gave you, and have considered your petition. And this is my decree. The Hebrews shall be allowed to leave Egypt and make their pilgrimage into the desert to serve their God; and as a further concession, their little ones shall go with them. Three whole days' grace shall be given them, then shall they return. None shall remain behind in Goshen during those three days, except only your flocks and your herds. Of them you will have no need."

And Moses answered the king: no longer as does a suitor pleading for a monarch's favours, but as one who makes terms with the vanquished.

"Pharaoh in his wisdom is pleased to make sport of his suppliant," he said. "For how shall Israel make solemn sacrifice to the Lord if our sheep and our cattle remain in Goshen? They too shall go with us, and not a hoof be left behind. For not until we come to the place that the Lord has appointed shall we ourselves know what he will require of us. Ay, and thou thyself must give us beasts, the choicest of thine own herds, for the feast that Israel shall make in the wilderness, and these of his mercy shall be accepted of thee as a peace-offering to the Lord our God."

Pharaoh rose from his throne, blinded to reason, his face transfigured with fury.

"Must and shall," he cried, "are these thy threats! Get thee gone; and take heed to thyself! Enter my presence no more. For on the day thou seest my face again thou shalt surely die."

Then said Moses: "So be it. Thou hast spoken well. I will see thy face again no more. Nay, not until thou thyself send for me in irremediable terror and despair. But I have a word for thee before I go. Hearken to it!

"Thus saith the Lord. Again and again we have made our humble petition to thee, according to his word, and thou hast scorned and defied him. Thou hast been warned, and not once but many times have the justice and might of the God of Israel been revealed to thee. Yet when thou didst show any shadow of relenting and didst plead for mercy, his mercy was vouchsafed to thee. But now, this is the end.

"There comes a midnight, and that soon, when the God of Israel will manifest himself yet once again; and thy heart shall melt in thee like water, for the anguish that is come upon thee. But thou shalt relent too late. In that night the angel of death shall wing his way from one end of Egypt to the other, from the mountains even to the sea, and when all the land is hushed in sleep he will smite the first-born of every household in Egypt from the highest to the lowest. From the prince himself, thy eldest son, even to the first-born of the slave woman who grinds corn at the mill—none shall escape. There shall go up to heaven that night such a cry of lamentation throughout all the land of Egypt as has never been heard before, and shall never be heard again.

"But in Israel shall be peace and safety. Nor shall one of the least of her children come to harm. So serene shall be that night in Goshen that not even a dog shall lift its tongue and howl in menace of woe against the moon. And by this thou shalt know that the Lord hath set his seal upon his chosen, and made a severance between the Egyptians and Israel. Yea, and one word more. In that day the proudest nobles and counsellors that stand about thy throne shall come in grief and horror of mind and prostrate themselves before me and make obeisance, even to me, entreating Israel to be gone and to return to Egypt no more. Then, and not until then, will I lead God's people forth."

Moses turned away from before the throne, and in the gloom of the vast gilded hall no voice answered him, nor was any attempt made to stay or molest him. And he went out from Pharaoh hot with anger.

The Feast of the Passover

He returned to Goshen. He knew that the long conflict of mind and will with Pharaoh was at an end. In the presence of his nobles and counsellors he had not only defied him face to face, but had forewarned him of a calamity with which the judgments that had already befallen Egypt would be as dust in the balance, and which would pierce the king himself to his very heart.

No further parleyings with Pharaoh were now conceivable. They were only once to meet again. And though not even the most headstrong and violent of the king's advisers might dare counsel the king to arraign or destroy Moses openly, there were other methods of ridding Egypt of its enemies. Moses knew well that from this day forward his life would be in unceasing danger. But he gave no thought to it.

Since he had returned from his quiet and serene existence as a shepherd with Jethro the priest of Midian, he had known no release from care. Each day that passed had brought its own ordeal. But his diffidence and self-distrust had left him. He was filled with a great weariness, but his spirit was unshaken. He had come back to his own people after many years' absence; and few had remembered him. Fewer still among the chief men of Israel had not in the long struggle wavered in their trust in him as their leader.

But now, though to all intents he might seem as yet to have failed in his mission, not only was his name a thing of dread in Egypt, but he was beloved and renowned among his own people, and he was hailed throughout Israel as the herald sent from the Eternal to free them from their woes.

When doubt assailed him, he had spent long hours of meditation in solitude on the fringes of the desert. In that silence, broken only by the night-cries of beast and bird, he had watched the stars wheel onward to their setting, and in a voiceless communion of heart and soul he had learned all that the Lord God would require of him. He cast all thought of himself from out of his mind, and laboured fearlessly on in ardour for Israel. And he knew that the day of deliverance was at hand.

He called together the elders. They met by stealth and after nightfall, and Moses laid before them all that had passed during his last audience with the king. He warned them that in his fury Pharaoh might decree inhuman reprisals against the Hebrews to avenge the humiliation he had endured in the presence of his courtiers. He might endeavour by every crafty means he could devise to incite them to open revolt. But they must endure in patience whatever the day might bring forth. They must be strong and resolute; they must trust in the Lord God of Israel.

Egypt's pride was soon to be broken; for what had now been demanded of the king was no longer a mere three days' truce from their quarries and brick-yards, but a release for evermore. They were about to set out on a journey from whence there would be no turning back. Jehovah would scatter his enemies, and Israel would go free. Canaan, the land of promise, their predestined home—this must be the vision continually before their eyes. The whole world should hear that they were no longer a captive and helpless race enslaved by a tyrant, but a nation free among nations, the chosen people of God.

Many of those who listened were old men wasted with age and weariness. From childhood their days had been spent in a cowed and hopeless servitude. The lash had been their wages; sleep their only refuge from misery; and death their one assurance of release. Yet they had lived on and suffered and endured.

Others among them were in the flower of their strength and manhood, lean, scarred and ravaged with toil, hollow of cheek, but fierce-eyed, fanatical and on fire with hatred of their oppressors. And they too sat motionless and intent.

One and all, they had listened in silence, and, except for the fleeting looks upon their faces and the light that burned in their eyes, had showed no sign of what was passing in their minds.

But in the pause that followed, there rose up from among them a murmur, a sigh, of joy and longing beyond all speech. The radiance of a hope no longer faint and far had broken in upon them as if with the light of the risen sun. Tears coursed down their cheeks, furrowed with woe and despair. They bowed their heads and worshipped.

But there were still many things to be considered, and many questions to be answered. They debated earnestly together and far into the night, and when at length the assembly broke up, and they went out silently into the darkness every man to his own place, their plans for the days that followed had been prepared. They had made a solemn vow to obey in everything the will of the Lord God, as Moses had revealed it. In sure and certain hope of their deliverance, and at the hour appointed, the host of Israel was to be in readiness, and none should remain behind.

By evening of the next day every man in Israel knew that the day of deliverance was soon to dawn and how he himself was to prepare for it. Yet these glad tidings had been spread abroad with such caution and secrecy that not a rumour of them reached the ears of the Egyptian overseers or the masters of the gangs.

Now, until this time, the beginning of the Hebrew year had been in the first month of harvest. But henceforward, as Moses had proclaimed to the elders, it was to fall in the earliest month of spring. The night on which he had called them together was that of the vernal new moon. It had been ordained therefore, for an everlasting memorial of the year now before them, that this was to be accounted their New Year's Day.

Moreover, it had long been the custom in Israel to keep sacred the day when the moon of springtime shines like snow in the heavens, and to share together in a feast, as happy as their wretched state would admit, in honour of the Lord. Two weeks—and two weeks only—were yet to run before the first new moon of Israel's New Year would come to its fulness, and the feast they were then to share in joy and solemnity would far excel any that had ever gone before. It was to be prepared for therefore with scrupulous care, since the Lord God himself had appointed it for a remembrance to all Israel.

The days passed heavily by. Midnight followed midnight. The sun rose and sank to his setting in skies continually windless and serene. The horned crescent of the moon appeared in the dying light of evening, and increased in the lustre it borrowed from the sun. So perfect a calm reigned in the heavens over Egypt, after the horrors of storm and tempest, whirlwind and darkness, that Pharaoh and the counsellors who concurred with his policy began to console themselves with the belief that all trouble with the abhorred Hebrews was now at an end.

On the night after Moses had last appeared before him the king had striven in vain to compose himself to sleep. The imprecation that Moses had uttered against him rang on in his ears, like the knelling of a bell, and in spite of an outward indifference, he had been so much moved by it that he had given command to his most trusted servants to keep unceasing watch over the prince, his firstborn.

But as dawn succeeded dawn, and his son was restored to him again safe and well, and no evil omen had shown itself to those who had kept watch within and without his chamber, his spirit revived in him. He began to upbraid himself, and even to mock a little at his fears. Though never within memory had Egypt suffered so grievously, though the state of his realm and people was a cause for grave disquiet, how could it be proved beyond doubt, he questioned within himself, that this was due to divine retribution? And even if it were so, it seemed that the God of the Hebrews had wearied of his demands.

He smiled, the dark eyes in his lean cavernous face fixed in reverie, as he pondered how best to contrive the death of their insolent leaders, to defame even their memory in the eyes of their own people, and to quell without mercy but at not too great a cost—for the life even of a slave had its price —any disorder or revolt that might follow.

But though Pharaoh could thus deceive himself, the apprehensions of the wiser of his counsellors were not so easily allayed. Though, too, at threat of instant vengeance the king himself had given command that no word of what had passed during the last audience he had granted to Moses should be whispered abroad, rumour of it had spread far and wide, and had filled the people with terror of an impending doom.

The Hebrews were now feared as much as in former times they had been hated and despised, and those of the Egyptians who lived in touch with them, and the dwellers in the Egyptian city of Psapt that was in Goshen, sought by every means in their power to placate them with gifts and bribes. Nothing that the Hebrews asked of them, and they asked freely as Moses himself had bidden them, was refused. They accepted these things not as an indulgence but as a right, wages long owing for the evils they had suffered and their centuries of toil.

As ordained by Pharaoh, his overseers and taskmasters

had cruelly increased the labour and the torments of the Hebrew gangs that worked under them, until they were almost beyond human endurance. But the old sullenness and apathy had vanished. Some divine secret hope seemed now to make their sufferings of no account. They toiled on as if all resentment had been clean forgotten.

An ancient song of Canaan, wild and plaintive and sweet, had spread from mouth to mouth. To the Egyptians it was meaningless, and yet as they hearkened, a hidden menace jarred its strains. It haunted them and they feared the sound of it. But when even speech was forbidden between slave and slave, by the light on their faces they seemed to be still singing in their hearts. A hush of dread and expectancy was over the land.

On the tenth evening of the new Hebrew year so brightly shone a great gibbous moon that the light of day waned without interval of darkness into the light of night. On this day, as Moses had commanded through the elders, every householder in Israel had set apart from among his few sheep or goats a lamb or a kid of one year old, the best he had, the first-born of its mother, and without any defect or blemish. This too was a sacred symbol, for ever afterwards the first-born among Israel were to be accounted sacred to the Lord.

This first-born lamb was intended for the feast that was to be partaken of by himself and his whole household four days afterwards, the feast day appointed by the Lord. And if any household, owing to the fewness of its members or its children, were too small to need a lamb for its own use only, it was to share one with its neighbour.

That day, longed for beyond all telling, dawned at length. The Hebrews set out as usual from their quarters to the brickyards, the quarries and the great temple that was then in building. It was a day of furious heat, airless and ominous. The overseers of the gangs, fearful of laying before Pharaoh misgivings so vague that they could find no proof of them, were nevertheless convinced that the Hebrews were secretly plotting against them, and barbarously drove them on. Many swooned with exhaustion by the way, and died, untended, where they fell. But no cruelty devised either by hatred or terror could now extort from the Hebrews a single rebellious word or action: not even so much as a groan of pain or of weariness.

At length the sultry hours drew towards evening, and the gangs were dismissed from their toil. For the last time the hewers of stone laid aside their picks and their mallets, and the makers of bricks their water-skins, their shovels and moulds; and all turned homeward. The gangmasters and overseers withdrew to their own quarters; and the quarries and works, where never more was any son of Israel to be seen at slavish toil again, lay idle in the wild colours of the declining sun.

At the brief hour that comes between sunset and the dark every householder in Goshen took the lamb that he had set apart and slaughtered it for the feast. Then he dipped into its blood a bunch of hyssop or marjoram—a wild, sweet, aromatic herb that grew freely on the walls of almost every dwelling in Goshen—and he sprinkled the blood on the door of his house, on its posts and on its lintel. The doom foretold to Moses by Jehovah was at hand. The angel of death, whose face is veiled, would be abroad in Egypt that night, and no human dwelling would be spared from his visitation except only those thus sprinkled, its door shut and made fast. From this moment until the hour appointed by Moses, no man in Goshen ventured abroad; none went out and none came in.

When night fell, a profound quietude lay over the settlements of the Hebrews. The dewy moon-bright air was chill and sweet with springing grass and flower. No light gleamed out from any window of the mean black hovels walled with sun-baked mud. Every door was shut—its posts and lintel stained dark with blood.

But within those walls was a continual stir and business. The whole long day had been spent by the woman of the household in preparing for the night. Nothing she treasured or might need was to be left behind, except only what was too heavy or cumbersome to be carried away. When the lamb had been skinned and dressed and made ready, she set it down to roast at the fire, whose ruddy glow illumined the narrow walls.

Flat cakes and biscuits without yeast or leaven (for nothing that had any taint of corruption was to have any part in the feast) had already been kneaded and now were baking. Bitter herbs—wild lettuce, endive and nettle—for symbol of the long sufferings of Israel, had been gathered and cleansed for a salad. She did all that she had to do with the utmost care, having provided as far as possible only as much food as would be eaten that night, for no remnant of this sacred meal was to be left over until the following morning. Whatever remained unconsumed was to be burnt in the fire.

An hour before midnight, all was ready. The children of the house, who had been sent early to bed, were woken from sleep, and everyone within it, even the little ones but lately out of arms, gathered together to partake of the feast. In years gone by this moon-bright harvest festival had been held with rejoicings. They had sat down to eat, drink and be merry at leisure, and had for the time being almost forgotten their misery. There had been no need then for haste or secrecy.

But this—both the first breaking of their fast this fourteenth night of Spring, and their last anxious supper in the land of their captivity—was no ordinary feast. It was the most solemn hour in the long history of their race—a token that from that day forward Israel had dedicated its firstborn to the service of God. Since by his mercy, on this disastrous night for Egypt, the angel of death was to spare and pass over the people of all Israel, the feast was to be called the *Feast of the Passover of the Lord*. And his divine influence would be shed on all who took part in it, worn-out in body, deadened in soul, and brutalized though many of them were.

They ate standing, the men of the household with their girdles about their loins, their sandals on their feet, and staff in hand; the women and children in whatever clothes could be provided that would shield them against the cold of the night air in the darkness of the desert. Few words were spoken. Their hearts were too full for speech. They longed for, yet dreaded the ordeal that lay before them. These hovels, mean and squalid though they were, had been their homes. They were to see them no more. They pined for the tents of the wanderer, but they were to venture out into the dread unknown and on a pilgrimage from which there could be no turning back. Who could foresee what dangers and what foes were waiting for them in the drear wastes of the wilderness—the resort, as they had heard, of monstrous beasts and evil demons, with hollow voice and secret music, luring to destruction the unwary and the lost?

Yet there were few among them who did not steadfastly believe in the wisdom and genius of their great leader, or doubted that he had been divinely chosen to set them free. But Pharaoh was mighty and merciless. Death or maiming or torture was the punishment he meted out to his enemies who defied him. How many of their own harmless babes had the Nile swallowed up in its infested waters! And as they looked at their children gathered round them, an icy horror shook them at the thought of the judgment of God soon to be revealed against Egypt, which even the tyrant king himself could not escape.

Astonished at being roused from sleep at so late an hour and at sharing in a supper that seemed as strange and marvellous as a dream, the younger children in hushed voices questioned their father about what they did, and why they were going out in the middle of the night, and where they were going to.

He gathered them around him. It was a feast, he told them, which even they themselves had been expressly bidden to share in by the Lord God. He spoke to them of Canaan also, a little land lying between wilderness and sea, only fifteen days' slow burdened journeying from north to south, only ten from east to west, yet a land wondrously rich in vineyard and orchard, mountain, valley, pasture and well-springs, its vales marvellously fair and sweet with flowers at this season of the year. A land flowing with milk and honey, their earthly paradise, the haven where they longed to be.

There, in the vale of Hebron, before he had been sold to the Ishmaelites, Joseph himself had lived as a child with Jacob his father who loved him. This was the land that, long time gone, had been promised of God not only to Jacob but to his father Isaac also, and to Abraham before him, who had worshipped him in faith and hope.

And now, after all these years of Israel's woes and slavery, they themselves, children with all their lives before them, were about to set out on a journey to a place of peace and refuge for which those who were at rest in their graves had pined in vain with a heartsick longing. In time to come when they had grown up to be men and women, and when, with each returning Spring they kept again this solemn feast, their own children also would question them as they themselves had questioned him.

By then, it might be, the doings of this strange night would be no more than a faint, far memory in their minds. Let them strive then with all their might to keep it clear and vividly in remembrance, so that in their turn they should be able to tell their children all this feast had meant to them, and the wonders that had gone before, and would yet be revealed. Let it be to them for a lifelong token in their hearts; let them bind its remembrance like a frontlet between their brows.

The children listened, their eyes shining, their hearts wildly beating. They promised their father to do all that he had bidden them do, and to keep all that he had said in remembrance.

So, throughout Goshen this, the first feast of the Passover, was being kept; and all Israel was awake and ready.

The Flight from Egypt

The moon rode high in the heavens above Egypt, smiting with its silver the wide waters of the Nile, and glazing as if with hoar-frost the walls of her temples and palaces and the slabbed sides of her prodigious pyramids. There slept the kings who centuries before had built them as their last resting-place, trusting, though vainly, that their mummied bodies in the long darkness between this world and the next would never be disturbed.

Ink-black shadow chequered the streets, the idle quarries, and the brickyards that all day long had been astir like a swarming nest of ants. Except for the watchmen in her frontier forts and desert camps, and the sentries who kept guard over the palace and armouries of Pharaoh, the whole realm of Egypt lay hushed in sleep. In his own royal city the howl of a dog, the footfall of some homeless prowler or of one abroad in trouble or on an urgent errand, and the far yell of wolf or hyæna, prowling on the outskirts of the wilderness, were the only sounds that broke the silence.

Few stars blazed in the windless heavens, except those that, rising or setting, hung low on the earth's horizon. They were quenched in the glare of moonlight that flooded the skies. At the approach of midnight, the whole land of Egypt, transfigured with loveliness, lay dazed as if entranced. But the avenging angel had gone his way; and the silence was not only the silence of sleep but of death.

At midnight cockcrow, lamps began suddenly to shine and flit in the dusky moonlit gloom within the dwellings of the Egyptians and to gleam from their windows. Doors were flung open. Cries of grief and horror pierced the hush, and were echoed on from house to house, from court to court. The wide high streets where stood temple and palace and the mansions of the wealthy, and every narrow by-way were suddenly thronged with a multitude of people, demented with anguish, seeking help and finding none.

Tidings of the woeful calamity that had befallen them

spread on from mouth to mouth. And with every moment, terror not only of the known but of the unknown pierced some poor human breast.

Stark and shivering with dread, the attendants whom Pharaoh had appointed to keep watch over his first-born entered his chamber and roused him from sleep. He started up out of his dreams as if at the touch of a spectre. Prostrating themselves before him, with tears and groans, they told him that the son he loved lay stricken and lifeless upon his bed. He gazed at them, his high-boned narrow face wan and lank and vacant, as if, though he had heard the words they uttered, his mind were incapable of understanding them.

He questioned them, and shook as if with the palsy when he realized the full meaning of the news they brought him. And he rose up in the night, he and all his servants and all the Egyptians, and there was a great cry in Egypt, for there was not a house without its dead.

His statesmen and his counsellors were sent for. All was confusion. They came into his presence, misery on their faces and grief in their hearts.

In the depth of night messengers were dispatched to Goshen urgently summoning Moses and Aaron. They were brought at once into the presence of the king, the women and servants of the palace who met them on their way fleeing in terror at sight of them.

The palace was loud with their wailings and the lamentations of the mourners. The bright moon shone in upon its gilded stones, and the nobles, assembled there in attendance on the king, after one glance at these Hebrews, averted their eyes. Pharaoh himself came down from his dais and advanced as if to meet them in the midst.

But a few paces from them he stayed, his face stricken

with woe, mutely scrutinizing them, and advanced no nearer. He spoke like a man almost bereft of his senses.

"I have summoned you hither," he said, "only that I may speak with you face to face. Pay heed to me now as you hope to be heeded of God. Tarry not for the morning but gather together all the people of Israel and lead them out of Egypt. Let them leave nothing that is theirs behind them, neither their children nor their flocks nor their herds, nor anything they own or need.

"Go," he said, "and serve the Lord your God, even as you have said it is required of you." He turned, stooping, then raised his haggard face and looked earnestly on Moses. "As for thee," he said, "I entreat thee to give me thy blessing in the mercy of thy God, for the bitterness of death is come upon me."

He commanded that all things that might be required should be given to the elders without stint, and that Moses himself should be obeyed in everything as he might direct. Word was instantly sent to every household in Israel. And all were in readiness.

They divided what they had to carry away with them between those who could bear it best. Their beasts of burden were already fed and watered, saddled and laden. They took the raw dough they had prepared for baking, they wrapped up their kneading-bowls in the woollen mantles they wore upon their shoulders, and which would serve them as a covering by night. They gathered their children together, and with their asses, their flocks and their herds, assembled in companies, each man in the place that had been appointed him beforehand, under his own chief or elder.

Though the moon gave light in abundance, torches flared; the night was thronged with their host. And the Egyptians—those who dwelt round about Goshen and in its chief city—far from attempting to stay or hinder them in their flight, urged them on. They left their dead, and with terror knocking at their hearts, adjured the Hebrews to intercede between them and the vengeance of Jehovah. Throughout their lives these Hebrews had been reviled and scorned and hated. Now the Egyptians loaded them with gifts and whatever might prove of service to them. They bribed them with their most precious possessions—jewels of silver and jewels of gold, vessels and fine raiment, their earrings, amulets, bracelets, and golden fillets. Their one desire was only to persuade and to incite them to be gone. "Else," they cried one to another, "we be all dead men!"

At break of dawn on the fifteenth day of the first month and in the springtime of this their first new year appointed by Moses, the whole host of Israel, men, women and children, in their thousands, and in their clans and tribes, began their march. They went up armed and with a high hand out of Egypt. And a multitude went with them—Egyptians who had intermarried with them, and prisoners taken in the frontier wars who had shared in the labours of the slave gangs. The earth shook with their tramping, and the cold air of daybreak was filled with the bleating and bellowing of their flocks and cattle and the sound of their chantings as they marched on.

Thus was fulfilled the vision which comforted Jacob when he dreamed that night long gone at Beersheba on his journey into Egypt. So Joseph himself had foreseen and foretold in the hour that comes before death. Nor was the solemn oath that had been sworn to him forgotten. All these years his bones—Pharaoh's ring upon his finger, the necklet of gold on his breast—had lain close-swathed and embalmed in spices in the painted and gilded coffin that had been prepared for him by the most skilful of the embalmers in the service of the king, his master. The bearers chosen by Moses himself lifted it from its abiding-place in Goshen and bore it away, to keep it in safe charge until they should come at length into Canaan, the land of his desire. There to lay it to rest for ever in Shechem, in the tomb that had belonged to his father Jacob.

They pressed on—an exceeding great multitude—by way of the long, narrow, cultivated strip of land that lay eastward of Goshen; from Rameses on to Succoth or Pithom, the great cities which the Hebrews themselves had built during their long bondage in Egypt. Thus they followed the canal of fresh water between the Nile and the sea which had been made by the Pharaoh who ruled Egypt when Moses was a child. It was a full four days' journey. Each nightfall they pitched their camp, and with every dawn prepared to continue on their way. They made what speed they could, but were compelled to keep pace with their flocks and herds, and were encumbered with heavy burdens.

And the angel of the Lord went before them, by day in a pillar of cloud to show them the way, and by dark in a pillar of fire to give them light. Thus was the angel of the Lord continually their beacon, by day and by night, in cloud or fire.

From Succoth they pressed on to Etham, which lay on the borders of the wilderness of that name. There again they pitched their camp and rested.

The direction in which they were now marching would bring them, if persisted in, to the coast of the Great Sea. Here was the ancient highway followed by the caravans between Egypt and Gaza, and by the armies of Pharaoh, and it was guarded by fortresses and strongholds against the attacks of marauders.

And the word of the Lord came to Moses, bidding him turn back from Etham, lest the men of Israel, unused as yet to war, might fear to go forward. Next morning, therefore, when they had eaten and made ready, they turned southward towards the wilderness or desert that lies to the east between Egypt and the Red Sea. And Moses led them by way of Pi-hahiroth where was the sanctuary of Osiris, the Sun-god of Egypt, and which lay on the coast between Migdol and the sea towards Baal-zephon—a tower sacred to the tribes that dwelt near by. There, over against the shores of the leaden sea, they pitched their camp.

Throughout their march from day to day they had been closely watched. Spies had followed them, mingling with the throng, and had reported their every movement to Pharaoh and whatever else could be discovered of their secret plans. And when word was brought to him that the Hebrews had assuredly fled out of Egypt, with intent to free themselves for ever from his yoke, and that the whole host of them was now moving south towards the sea, then that evil genius in his mind which had led him on from one disaster to another, whispered within him that surely now he had them at his mercy.

Hatred of Moses blinded him to all else. Jehovah had done his worst; he feared him not. He put away his grief for his dead son, and thirsted only for revenge.

He summoned his chief officers and laid before them the reports that had been brought to him by his spies. "See now," he said, "these Hebrews, in their ignorant folly, are encamped near the watch-tower of Migdol, their aim, it is clear, being to follow the nearer shore of the sea which will entangle them in at length between its tides and the mountains. Surely this god they worship has abandoned them. We have them in our power, and may be avenged on them

[205]

once and for all for the evil they have brought upon Egypt. They shall drink bitterly of the might of Pharaoh and shall cry, 'Woe! woe on us, for the day that we were born!' "

Those of his counsellors who were as stubborn and stiff-necked as himself acclaimed his decision. And he made ready his chariot, and he mustered his army, and set it in array—his helmed footmen with lance and shield, his archers with their bows and hatchets, his horses and his chariots; his whole power and strength. And he made ready to march.

But first, for vanguard of his army he dispatched six hundred of his chariots with their charioteers and bowmen, bidding the captain in command of them spare neither horse nor man until he had come in sight of the Hebrews, and had brought them to bay. These, then, pressed on in hot pursuit, leaving Pharaoh himself with his main army to follow after them. And all that day they drew steadily nearer, while still the Israelites were encamped near the sea strand.

Towards evening, scouts of the Israelites who had been sent out by Moses to keep watch beyond the camp and to give warning if danger threatened, distinguished afar off across the sands of the desert the faint clouds of dust raised by Pharaoh's pursuing chariots, the vanguard of his army. And a heavy rumour of sound was borne on the air towards them like distant thunder. They stood transfixed, intent and listening.

But their ears had not deceived them. It seemed the distant tramplings even loudened as they hearkened, and the dust cloud of the chariots showed no changes as do the vapours of evening. They turned instantly and fled back into the camp, for lo, Egypt was marching after them, and they were sore afraid.

The Crossing of the Red Sea

Their report ran like wildfire from one end of the camp to the other, and it was seized with panic terror. These men of Israel, born into slavery and forced their whole lives long to toil for a tyrant, were unused to any discipline except that of the lash and the goad. They had no knowledge or experience of warfare. They were hampered with their flocks and herds already spent by forced marches, and were burdened with a vast hoard of baggage. Only the open spaces of the wilderness lay around them, even to the sea, and there was nowhere any place of defence for their women and children. When they knew that the dreaded armies of Pharaoh were in pursuit of them, their hearts melted like water. And in their despair they cried to the Lord.

But there were some among them who had been compelled to accept Moses as their leader against their will, men by nature rebellious, malcontents. They forced their way into the presence of Moses and reproached him bitterly for the mortal danger into which he had brought them.

"Was it", they reproached him, "because there were no graves for us in Egypt that thou hast enticed us out to die in the wilderness? Why hast thou so dealt with us, compelling us to flee out of Goshen; ay, and our helpless women and children? There at least our lives were safe. When thou didst first return to Goshen and began to incite us to revolt against the king, did we not again and again adjure thee to leave us alone that we might continue our labours in peace and security? Were we the only slaves in Egypt? Is Pharaoh to be cheated of what is his? Far better to live in the vilest bondage under the Egyptians than to die here in misery and our bones bleach in the sands of the wilderness!"

Moses faced them without wavering. Nor did he answer them in anger, nor reproach them for their faint-heartedness.

Far more clearly than they, he knew the supreme danger that now threatened them, and the massacre and horror that would follow if he swerved for an instant from his authority over them. He needed time to consider: but he remained steadfast and unmoved.

"Fear not," he adjured them, "but stand fast. Every man in readiness and unafraid. And you shall see the salvation of the Lord. It shall be revealed to you this very day. Believe only in Jehovah, the Lord God himself, whose wonders you have seen in Egypt. He has seen fit that this Pharaoh should harden his heart even yet again, to pursue after Israel. Blind and stubborn, this proud king believes in his folly that Jehovah hath forsaken us, and that we know not which way to escape, being shut in between the desert and the sea. Watch and wait! For it is Pharaoh himself who shall be taken in a snare, and the Lord shall have glory over him, and all Egypt shall know that he is the Almighty. For I vow unto you that these warriors of Pharaoh, the dust of whose chariots beclouds the skies, you shall see again no more for ever. Jehovah himself shall fight for you, if only you have faith and hold your peace."

He went out alone from among them, and continued on his way until he came down to the margin of the sea whose full flood-tide now lapped its sands. The waste of waters

stretched out before him; and there in solitude, his face towards the distant land of Canaan, that he himself was to see
but never tread, he prayed, wrestling in agony of soul for
the safety of Israel. The sweat stood on his face as he bowed
himself in entreaty before the Lord.

But peace at length calmed heart and mind; he was comforted and rose up. It was the hour of the setting of the sun,
and even the eastern verges of the horizon to which he
raised his eyes were inflamed with its last beams. The whole
ample canopy of the heavens was lit with wondrous light
and colour, ever changing, melting, its fires mounting, to
fade and die with night. He lifted up his hands over the sea
in enraptured salutation of the Eternal whom he worshipped. Then in the swift cold oncoming of the dark he
returned back into the camp.

The pillar of cloud, that had gone on before the host of
Israel, had removed and now stood kindled between the
starry skies and the wrath behind them. Between the huge
straggling host of the Israelites and the pursuing vanguard
of the armies of Pharaoh, there settled a region of dense
gloom—illumined, like the smoke of a burning mountain,
by the sombre pillar of fire that was the abiding-place of the
angel of the Lord.

Perplexed, and apprehensive of what this unearthly ap-
parition in the heavens might portend, the captain in command of the chariots sent out scouts to reconnoitre. They
faded from view in the mounded obscurity of the desert,
but only one of them returned to him alive, wounded and
terrified, and with nought but his tongue-stump wherewith
to speak. Pharaoh's urgent orders in mind, the captain of
the vanguard hesitated, but at length, after consultation
with his officers, and confident that he had the Hebrews in
his power, since their flight was now cut off by the sea, he

determined to advance no further in the darkness, but to attack at dawn. His men and his horses were hard spent and needed a brief respite. All that long night the Egyptians drew no nearer.

But with sunset a wind from between east and north had begun to rise, trumpeting mournfully between earth and sky. In the cold of the dark it steadily increased in force and at last grew exceeding strong. It roared under the night, burdened with whispering sand, beneath a sky wildly brilliant with stars, and, in the small hours, lit with the beams of a waning moon.

Sleep came but fitfully to those huddled together about their watch-fires. The women lay in terror of the tumult, clasping their little ones to their breasts, soothing their cries. Yet this was the wind of their great mercy, for in its vehemency it drove back the tumultuous fast-ebbing tide of the sea towards the south-west until its very bed was exposed beneath the stars, and where had been water was now land.

Thus the wind continued to blow in the cloudless dusk of the now dwindling moonlight, and in the watch that comes before morning the whole host was aroused. Even the children who were old enough to walk and who had been slumbering peacefully, lapped warm against the cold, were awakened. And behold, when they looked out towards where at sunset had been the tumbling billows of the sea, there lay before them a mile-wide ford stretching across from shore to shore. The whole hidden desolate channel of the sea lay exposed, and beckoned them on.

The watch-fires of Israel had burned low, and were now heaped high with fuel, to deceive what spies might be lurking behind them. Strict orders had been given that all voices and sounds be hushed. In silence the men drew together in their ranks and companies, and at about the beginning of the last watch of the night they began to move forward. Leading on their timid flocks and their herds and their beasts of burden, they descended the gently sloping sands that had margined the flood-tide the night before, and advanced on to the wind-swept floor of the sea, its salty boulder-strown sands faintly glimmering in the moonlight and the wan of day.

Thus the whole multitude of Israel, with their women and their children in their midst, pressed onward. But for the occasional bleating and lowing of their beasts, the wailing of an infant and the plashing of foot and hoof in the oozy sands and shallow pools of brine between the rocks, they marched in a profound silence, marvelling as they went, and filled with a wild elation between joy and fear at this miracle of the Lord.

And when the main body of them had reached the eastern shore, then the rearguard who had kept watch on the western shore, followed after them with all dispatch. And in the first crystal of daybreak the pillar of cloud was seen to be in front of them in the wilderness beyond the sea. There they halted.

Roving tribesmen of the desert a little before dawn came to the commander of the chariots of Egypt to report this wonder. Utterly amazed and dismayed at news of it, he summoned his officers. The peril of Pharaoh's wrath was on their heads, they dared not pause or consider. The trumpets sounded; the charioteers and bowmen leapt to their stations; the horses were harnessed; the advance began. So translucent were now the eastern skies that even at this distance they could see afar off the faintly gleaming ensign or standard of Moses beyond the farther shore.

The sight filled them with fury. Urging on their horses with lash and cry, they pressed forward in their battalions at their utmost speed. Their iron rumblings shook the air. Else all was still; for the wind that had filled their ears with its hollow trumpetings throughout the night had fallen to calm.

And as the foremost chariots drew near to the seashore, the sun rose, dazzling clear in the stilled air of the morning. It showed for an instant its full orb of splendour above a louring accumulation of cloud that lay on the horizon in the south-eastern quarter of the heavens.

But only for a moment, for the clouds mounted swiftly up after it into the skies, borne on by lofty winds, and now far below them a hot breeze of the desert began to stir, whipping the sand into scurrying whirls and puffs, that swept up like the dancing of phantoms, then fell to earth again.

Having come to hightide-mark on the sea-shore, the charioteers made no pause, but drove on furiously into the bed of the sea, following the pitted track from shore to shore left by the multitude of Israel. But the silt was sodden, the advance slow, and they strove in vain to keep rank and order. Daylight now had dimmed, for clouds were massed on high and obscured the zenith. The morning was black with storm.

And the angel of the Lord looked down from out of the pillar of cloud upon the chariots of the Egyptians. And the angel of the Lord in his splendour troubled and discomfited the Egyptians. Lightnings rent the gloom, and the thunder thundered, with torrents of rain. And when they were come into the midst of the bed of the sea, the wheels of their clogging chariots sank deep into the soft sand, so that they drave heavily. The horses, flecked with foam and affrighted, reared, plunged and stumbled; some bared their teeth and whinnied; and many of the pins that held wheel to axle were snapped asunder, and the wheels fell away. And now,

however wildly the leading charioteers, with their stooping
bowmen, lashed and shouted, they made but little progress;
and they were dazed and confused by the tumult of the
storm.

And some among them, who feared the power of Moses
and the wrath of God, were suddenly seized with terror and
turned back in their tracks, crying "Away! Back! Away!
The Gods are against us! Jehovah fights against us!"

But still those in the rear continued to press on. And in
this mellay they struggled one against another in fury and
consternation in the midst of the bed of the sea, their hearts

pierced with dread of they knew not what danger, their one desire being to regain dry land and flee back away into Egypt. But still their captains urged them on.

Then Moses in the presence of Israel stretched forth his hand toward the sea. And behold there sounded out of the distance—above the din and tumult of the rain and thunder, and the shouts of the charioteers—the roar of water. In a liquid wall of crystal its lightning-lit torrent swept surging back into its customary channel. The Egyptians heard; they turned faces haggard with fear, and knew in their souls the doom that was upon them. But too late; snowy with foam the sea, in its course and strength, swept down upon them in one vast billow, and returned into its bed. Its waves met over them, and submerged them in the deeps, and not one of them remained alive.

Thus the Lord God saved Israel that day from the vengeance of Pharaoh and the armies of Egypt; and the corpses of the charioteers were flung up by the tide of the sea before their eyes, and the sea-shore was strown with their dead. And all Israel was filled with awe and wonder. They believed in their inmost hearts in the Lord, and in his faithful servant Moses, and rejoiced with an exceeding great joy.

In the peace that followed the storm Moses and Aaron and the elders of Israel gathered the people together in a solemn assembly.

And Miriam, the prophetess, took a timbrel in her hand, and the women of Israel went out after her with dancing and music, and sang to the Lord a song of joy and triumph and thanksgiving. And these were the words of the song they sang that day, while the people with their voices in their thousands on the shores of the sea took up the strains of it in mighty unison; and the firmament rang again:

I will sing unto the Lord, for he hath triumphed gloriously;
The horse and the rider hath he thrown into the sea.
The Lord is my strength, of him shall be my song.
Sing unto the Lord who alone is our salvation.
He is my God, to him will I give thanks,
The God of our fathers, and I will exalt him.
> *Mighty he in battles,*
> *Jehovah is his name!*
The chariots of Pharaoh hath he cast into the sea,
His captains and their hosts he hath whelmed in its waters.
> *They lie drowned in its deeps,*
> *They sank like a stone.*

Thy right hand, Lord Jehovah, is glorious in power,
Terrible in its might, confounding thy foes.
In the splendour of thy majesty thou didst shatter them that
    challenged thee,
As fire amid the stubble ran the flame of thy wrath.
Blast of thy nostrils, came the wind from out the south.
It gathered up the waters till they stood upon an heap,
And the floods were congealed in the heart of the sea.
Cried the foe in his pride, "I will chase and overtake,
Rich shall be the spoil I will seize and divide.
My soul shall be sated with destruction and plunder,
With unscabbarded sword I will glut my desire."
Thou didst blow with thy wind, and the wild wave covered them;
Their clanging chariots gurgling sank like lead into the deep.
O Lord Jehovah, what gods can be compared to thee?
Glorious and supreme, who is like unto thee?
Wondrous in holiness, and fearful in all mysteries,
Lo, now thy foes are foundered in the sea.
Compassionate in mercy, thou didst lead forth thy people.
'Tis thou in thy compassion who hast saved them and redeemed.

The nations of the earth they hear, they are afraid.
Pangs of fierce woe have seized the princes of Philistia;
The proud dukes of Edom are dumb with amaze;
The mighty men of Moab they shudder as they hearken;
The hearts of all Canaan melt away in fear.
Terror and astonishment have seized upon their chieftains,
Confounded with thy wonders, they sit stark as is a stone.
They shall watch, O Lord Jehovah thy people pass through
    them.
Thy people march on—thy redeemed and thy chosen.
Thou shalt bring them in and plant them in the mount of thine
    inheritance,
The place thyself hadst made to be to thee a dwelling;
The Sanctuary, O Lord, established by thy hands.

There the Lord shall reign for ever and for ever,
In the glory of his Kingdom, and world without end!

THE
WILDERNESS

The Death of Moses

Thus came Israel out of Egypt; and the armies of Pharaoh were to trouble them no more. But his hand was mighty and this blow to his pride bitter to bear. They made no delay therefore and set forward on their great pilgrimage. Even when there was nothing to impede or harass them, the movement of such a multitude was very tardy since the whole host was compelled to keep pace with the children and weaklings, their flocks and herds. They had but few beasts of transport and were heavily burdened, and the day's advance from one night's encampment to the next was a distance seldom more than five miles.

Their course at first lay through the desert of Shur or Etham, a region of shifting sands along the eastern shore of the uppermost reaches of the Red Sea, where there is little green pasture and well-springs of water are few. Beyond this desert lay the wilderness of Zin. Here they turned eastward and came to Rephidim where they defeated the tribesmen of Amalek who had raided and pestered them on their way, and strove to prevent them from reaching the sweet waters of Paran.

They then advanced, ever ascending, towards the mountains of Sinai, through a country well-watered and fertile with groves of palm trees and acacias, and thickets of thorn and willow, the feathery tamarisk and the bright-leafed myrrh.

And when Jethro, the priest of Midian, heard that the
Israelites were encamped at Sinai, forthwith he set out with
his daughter Zipporah and her two sons to welcome Moses.
And Moses went out to receive his father-in-law, and
bowed himself before him and kissed him, and they rejoiced to meet again. And Moses brought his wife and his
sons and Jethro to his tent, and there he told him of all that
had passed since their last farewell. And Jethro rejoiced for
all the goodness which the Lord had done to Israel. "Now
I know", he said, "that the God you worship is greater than
the Gods of Egypt and all gods beside." And he himself
offered up sacrifice, and they feasted together, Moses and
Aaron and the chief men of Israel.

By Jethro's wise counsel, seeing that the labour of govern-
ment and the dispensing of justice was too great a burden to
be borne by one commander, Moses chose out the ablest
men of Israel and made them leaders over the people, rulers
of thousands, rulers of hundreds, and of fifties and of tens.
And he made many laws and ordinances for the guidance
of the people and decreed the penalties and punishments of
any who should offend against them. In all small matters
the rulers he had chosen sat in judgment over the people.
Only causes of great moment and difficulty were brought
before Moses himself.

The day came when Jethro must return to his own people,
and he went his way. But the host of Israel remained encamped among the mountains of Sinai, amidst gigantic
precipices of granite and porphyry. And in their presence,
though they were forbidden to draw near beyond the
bounds set for them, Moses ascended the sacred mountain
called Horeb, on whose slopes, when he sat keeping Jethro's
sheep, he had seen the bush that had burned with flame yet
was not consumed—the glory of the angel of the Lord.

Alone upon its summit he communed with God, and the
utmost heights of the mountain were hidden in a veil of
flaming splendour, and the mountain quaked, with thunderings and lightnings. There Moses remained in communion with the Lord forty days and forty nights, and
there tablets of stone, inscribed with commandments for the
obedience of Israel, were committed to his charge.

And because he tarried there so long, the people were
afraid and began to murmur, believing that he had forsaken
them and would return no more. They abandoned their

faith in the Lord Jehovah. Even in the shadow of the mountain they gathered together the gold ear-rings worn by their wives and sons and daughters. And following the rites of the Egyptians who in the form of an ox worshipped a god named Ptah, Aaron himself set up the image of a golden calf. And on the morrow after it was made, they rose up early and offered sacrifice before it and prostrated themselves; and when they had made sacrifice, they sat down to feast, and rose up to dance and to chaunt wild songs before this golden calf, trusting in that for their salvation. . . .

Nevertheless it was during their wanderings in the wilderness that a great tent or pavilion was fashioned to be the Tabernacle of the Lord and an enduring memorial to Israel wherein they might make atonement for their souls. And all the people brought precious vessels and offerings for its service, the chiefs of the tribes their gems, their gold and silver and brass, and all who had much, according to their means. Fine linen, dyed blue and purple and scarlet, silk, fleeces of rams and skins, oil for the lights and spices for sweet incense: all these were brought to Moses for the sacred adornment of the tabernacle; and even the poorest among them gave not less than half a silver shekel.

Within the tabernacle stood the altar of sacrifice; and in an inner chamber, veiled with embroidered curtains and named the Holy of Holies, was laid up the Ark of the Covenant between the Lord and his people Israel. This was a chest or coffer of acacia wood overlaid with gold, and within it were the tablets of stone and other precious objects. It was the most sacred symbol in Israel.

The whole tribe of Levi was devoted to the service of the Lord; and Aaron, who was himself a Levite, was at this time High Priest, and his sons Nadab, Abihu, Eleazar and Ithamar, were priests who ministered under him. They had made solemn vows, and had been anointed and consecrated and in their charge was the tabernacle and all that was within it. There they burned incense before the altar, and watched over the Ark of the Covenant, and fed with oil the seven-lamped golden candle-stick that burned in the holy place. And there they made sacrifice.

When in its simple beauty and splendour the tabernacle was completed, the elders of Israel met together in solemn assembly. And the glory of the Lord descended upon it, filling it as with a cloud with his radiance. It was an assurance to Israel of his presence there. When the cloud was lifted from over the tabernacle, they continued their march; but when the cloud rested upon it they camped in the place where at that time they chanced to be, and remained encamped until the cloud was lifted. For this great pavilion with its embroidered veils and curtains was so constructed that these and its poles, its altar and the Ark of the Covenant, could be removed and borne on with them on their pilgrimage.

On the twentieth day of the second month of the second year after their escape from Egypt, the people of Israel left Horeb behind them and journeyed on through the mountainous gorges of the great and terrible wilderness of Paran until they entered the lowlands of Kadesh in the wilderness of Zin.

They were now nearing the southern borders of Canaan. Like a vision of paradise, hope and longing for it had been continually in their minds, the blessed goal of their long travail and afflictions. It was a country that no man among them had ever seen with his own eyes, and it was as yet strange to them and undiscovered. Twelve men were therefore chosen, one from each of the tribes, for a perilous venture. They were given orders to make their way across its frontier by stealth, and to spy out the land, whether it were good or bad, wooded or barren; what manner of people dwelt in it, their kings and chieftains, their cities and strongholds, the numbers of their armed men, their might and wealth.

After forty days' absence the spies returned into the camp at Kadesh, burdened with fresh figs and pomegranates which they had plucked from the trees, and a vine branch with a cluster of luscious grapes upon it so heavy that it had to be carried between two of them, slung upon a staff.

They appeared before an assembly of the chief men of Israel and made their report. They told how wondrously rich in corn and pasture was the land they had seen, its groves of olives, its vineyards and fig trees and its abundance of milk and honey, for they had ventured on into the vale where Jacob had dwelt awhile when Joseph was a boy. But they reported also of the walled cities they had watched or entered, and the strong natural defences of the land, the power of its kings and the people over which they ruled and their men of war. And last, they told of the Anakim, a race of giants, men of prodigious strength and stature, that dwelt in the region of Hebron.

Of the twelve spies only two, Caleb and Joshua, the son of Nun, incited the assembly to march forward at once to invade the land, trusting in God to give them the victory. The other ten, daunted and discouraged by what they had seen, enlarged only on the mortal perils of such an enterprise, and filled the assembly with such terror of what lay before them that they rose up and cried out against Moses, "Would to God we had perished in Egypt! Would to God we had laid down our lives in the wilderness! To advance further is only utter destruction—an evil death to us all and perpetual bondage for our women and children."

When Caleb strove to reason with them and to enkindle them with his own valour, they threatened to stone him where he stood. They plotted together to depose Moses, and to elect in his stead a commander who would lead them back into Goshen by the way they had come, choosing rather a life safe and secure but in miserable slavery under Pharaoh, than to risk their all for so rich an inheritance in sure trust that God would be with them.

So it had been continually. Even though in their dire need miraculous waters had flowed from the rock, and, when other food had failed them, they had been nourished as if from heaven by manna, the gift of providence in the wilderness—manna that was white as coriander seed and tasted like waters made of honey, and that must be gathered early in the cool of the morning ere the heat of the sun should corrupt it—yet in spite of these divine mercies and the wonders that had been revealed to them in Egypt, at every threat of danger or difficulty, dearth or pestilence, they had murmured against him or broken out into open revolt against their leaders. And the punishment of God had been heavy upon them.

And yet again; now, even though the Land of Promise was within but a few days' march of them, they lost all hope and faith. Fainthearted and irresolute, they were never of the same mind from one day to another. And the hordes of the Amalekites and the Canaanites descended upon them, defeated them in battle, and chased them back into the wilderness of Zin. There they abode many long years.

Thence at length Israel journeyed to Mount Hor, where, in the presence of Eleazar and Moses, Aaron the High Priest died and was buried. Thence, they pressed on, south-ward, through the valley of Elath that lay at the uppermost reaches of the eastern branch of the Red Sea, the Gulf of

Aquaba. And there they came to the ancient highway of the caravans journeying between Mecca and Damascus. Skirting east of Edom, because its king refused them passage through his territory, they entered the land of the Moabites, with whom at the time they dealt peaceably, for they were the descendants of Lot, the nephew of Abraham. And they entered the mountainous region of Nebo, sheer ramparts of naked rock, the colours of their peaks and gorges ever changing in the splendour of the sun as it changes its station in the skies from dawn till eve. And not far distant hence, the waters of the river Jordan flowed into the sea.

So at length they were come again to the very borders of Canaan. And Moses knew that his end was near. He spoke for the last time before the congregation of the elders. He uttered prophecy and gave them his counsel; and he blessed the people. Then he surrendered up the sceptre of Israel to Joshua and charged him to be strong, faithful and of good courage, since to him had been given the glory of leading Israel into the land which had been promised them of old.

When this was done, he himself, weary with age and feebleness but of an indomitable will, went up alone to the heights of Mount Pisgah. There in solitude he gazed out westward, beyond the turquoise-blue waters of the Salt Sea and the river Jordan, over the sand-coloured plain of Jericho, the city of palm trees, towards Canaan, whose wooded mountains and valleys lay spread out beneath him, in the last beams of evening, and to the utmost shores of the Great Sea. He knew that it was not the will of God that he himself should set foot within its borders. So, but in agony of mind, he had stood alone, gazing out over the waters of another sea, while the chariots of Egypt were approaching the rabble of his defenceless followers, and only a miracle could save them from the vengeance of Pharaoh. Now he was at peace in the assurance that all was well with Israel, their pilgrimage at an end. His soul was refreshed with this vision of the future, and he longed to take his rest.

There in solitude he died, the Lord God his comfort; and he was buried in a valley of Moab, though no man knows the sepulchre where he was laid.

The Fall of Jericho

For forty years the Israelites had wandered and sojourned in the wilderness, in its wastes of scorching sun by day, and bitter cold by night, and they had seen hard warfare. They had defeated Sihon, king of the Amorites, bearded men and hardy, and had slain him with all his host. They had invaded the land of Og, the King of Bashan, a monarch of mighty stature who ruled over sixty cities fenced with walls and with gates and bars, and whose throne was of wrought iron; and they had vanquished Balak and the five princes of Moab who had allied themselves with the tribesmen of Midian.

They burned their cities and destroyed their strongholds and captured a very great booty, with many thousands of sheep and oxen and asses. But hardships had been heavy upon them, and death had wasted them.

Of the grown men among them who had been upwards of twenty years of age when they crossed the Red Sea in their flight from Egypt, not one now remained alive. Many of them had been faithless or rebellious. They had died by the way, or had been slain in battle. But the youngest children, who with dream-ridden eyes had shared with their mothers and fathers in the first solemn midnight Feast of the Passover a whole lifetime ago, were now in the full vigour of manhood. And their own sons had grown up to be young men hardy and fearless. They too had suffered but had endured.

And Israel, though but a race of desert tribesmen, ill-armed and few in numbers by comparison with the great nations around them, from being little better than a cowed and unruly mob of fugitives, had become a doughty, resolute and disciplined people, fierce of spirit, implacable in battle, and under captains bold and valiant and skilled in war. They were now moreover a race united and at one; their hearts aflame with ardour for the one true God they worshipped, even though they could follow his will but stumblingly, and were aware of him but darkly and in part.

All Israel mourned for Moses thirty days, and when the days of their great mourning were over, they marched on from the mountainous region of Nebo and encamped about seven miles north-east of the mouth of the Jordan where it pours its waters into the Salt Sea. It is a region sere and sombre, and sunken lowest of any land on earth beneath the level of the oceans.

But about two days' march beyond and westward of it stood the rich city of Jericho. Strongly fortified, it reared its massive walls amidst the plain, between the river and the mountains of Canaan. And on its downfall hung the conquest of all that lay beyond.

That day Joshua sent out two men, spies, with orders to make their way by stealth into the city and glean what knowledge they could of its power in men and arms and engines of war, and the strength of its defences. They disguised themselves, crossed over the Jordan by one of its fords, and pressed on across the burning plain until, after the heat of the day, they neared the bright oasis in the desert in which at the foot of its hills the city lay. Here were gardens wildly green and sweet to eyes parched with the weary sands of the wilderness. Groves of palms and cypresses, and bowers of green orange trees in bloom—there too, hedges of budded thorn and aromatic tamarisk, gourd and cucumber and fig, and plenteous vineyards. A stream of marvellous clear water gushed forth from its well-spring in the hills, to brim pools darting with fish, and the moat about the walls—thence to spend itself in a hundred channels, refreshing the gardens in the plain. And many birds made music by the waterside, for it was the hour of their evensong.

The two spies rested here, in hiding. Never even in their dreams had they looked out upon a country so fair. Verily Eden itself might once have been found here. Here then they lay until the sun had set behind the mountains, and the light of day had swiftly ebbed out of the heavens. And a little before nightfall they rose up and made their entry into the city by its eastern gate.

Already dark was down, and since the streets of the city would soon be deserted and any chance wayfarer might arouse suspicion, they knocked at the door of a house that seemed to be open to travellers, to seek lodging for the night. A woman named Rahab dwelt alone in this house, and she herself opened to them. Scanning their faces in the light of the lamp she carried, she admitted them, asked their business, and made them welcome. She set bread and wine before them and left them to refresh themselves.

But though they knew it not, the chief watchman at the gate had seen them enter the city, and mistrusting them for the spies they were, had had them followed to the woman's house. When it was reported to the king of Jericho that two Hebrews were concealed in the city, he was greatly wroth. He commanded that they should be seized instantly and brought before him, and that his torturers should be in waiting.

There came anon, then, a guard of soldiers to Rahab's house and beat upon the door. Spying out on them from a window, she guessed on what errand they were come. She ran in haste to the two spies where they sat supping together, and warned them of their danger. "Follow me now, at once," she bade them, "and with all caution, for there is not a moment to lose." And she herself ran on before them and led them up on to the flat roof of her house, which was built upon the city wall and overlooked the plain beyond it. There she hid them, heaping over them bundles of flax which had been laid out in order, to be dried in the sun for the weaving of linen. She bade them lie close until she came again, and not so much as stir or whisper.

[231]

Then she ran down and opened to the guard; and when they questioned and threatened her, she told them that the two men they were seeking had indeed come to the house and had entreated lodging for the night. But as she knew not whence they had come or who they were, she had denied them, and had herself watched and seen them go out of the city a little before dark, while there was yet time and the gates were not shut.

"Whither they went then I cannot say," she said. "But they were spent and on foot and cannot have gone far. Pursue after them quickly and you will certainly overtake them."

The soldiers left her, and set off as they thought in hot chase of the spies towards the fords of the Jordan, with intent to cut them off before they could cross over, though by now it was dark and the moon had set. And the gates of the city were shut after them.

When all sound of them was stilled, Rahab shut to her door and barred it and returned to the spies on the roof. She called to them softly and they crept out of their hiding-place. And she told them why she had given them shelter and had not betrayed them to their enemies. Even at first sight of them, she said, she had pierced through the disguise they wore, and knew them to be spies and Hebrews. For dwelling as she did near the gateway of the city, which was continually thronged with travellers and strangers, she had long since heard the rumour of the approach of the hosts of Israel. She had heard moreover how the Lord God they worshipped had driven back the waters of the Red Sea for their salvation, confounding the hosts of Pharaoh; and what fate had overtaken the kings of the Amorites, Og and Sihon, when they had set themselves in array against them.

"Of a truth," she said, "as soon as we of the city heard

these things our hearts melted within us. The king and all his captains are sick with apprehension. Why else should his soldiers have come knocking here to seize two helpless strangers unless it be for fear of him that sent you? I am myself a sinful woman and of little account, yet I assuredly know and believe that the Lord God who wrought these marvels is the true God that reigns in heaven above and over all things on the earth beneath it, and that the walls and towers of Jericho are less than nought against them that believe in him and do his will."

She stayed, gazing into their faces in the thin sprinkled light of the stars that burned wildly in the skies above them, her eyes darkly luminous, her countenance pale and rapt with the eager motions of her mind and the ardour of her heart. "Wherefore then," she continued earnestly, "I beseech you to vow unto me by the living God that since I have showed you kindness, you also will show kindness to those whom I love, and will save the lives of my father and my mother, my brothers and sisters, in the day of evil, and deliver us from death. What power had I? What if the commander of the armies of Israel had sent out a thousand spies into the city and all had been taken and done to death—what would that have availed against your God, Jehovah? Seeing then that I have kept faith with you, I pray you keep faith with me also."

Then said the two spies: "Our lives for thine—if thou utter no word of why we came here or whither we go. We swear it unto thee. As in our need thou hast dealt truly and kindly with us, so in the day that Jehovah shall give us the victory will we deal kindly with thee."

She was comforted. And she stooped and peered down over the wall of the city to see if aught were stirring. The air was sweet with the mingled fragrance of the spring, and in the hush of night the voice of the water coursing in its channels rang clear and changeable. She turned to them eagerly, yet as though in the peace and silence, sorrowful thoughts had found entry into her mind.

"Come, now," she said. "All is quiet and there is none to overlook us." And she brought them down from the roof into a chamber below, and to a window that hung over the city wall, for her whole house was built high out on the great width of the wall. And she took a strong cord woven of scarlet and bound it fast to the beam of the window, while the two spies stood back watching her and intently listening. And while they waited, their eyes took in all that lay around them in the small light of her lamp, her loom, her hanks of bright-dyed yarn, and the cloth she had woven.

When all was ready for their departure, they spoke earnestly with her, so that everything should be clear between them, and nothing should miscarry when the day of reckoning came.

"It was close on nightfall", they said, "when we entered the city, and we looked but scantly about us. The streets are strange to us, and we know not where thy people dwell. When we are gone, visit them secretly, then, and bind them by oath to breathe not a word of anything thou shalt say to them. And when the city is besieged and the day of the assault is come, see that they all meet together in this house and that not one of them be absent. For assuredly in the heat and terror of battle there will be no help or hope for any found at large in the streets against the vengeance of Israel. Do this then, and let no man else hear of it. And when all thy family are come together, bind this scarlet cord in the window for a signal, so that we and our captains shall see it there, and shall know which house is thine. Thus only shall you all be saved. But if any that are with you venture out of the doors of this house into the streets, then he goes at his own risk; and we ourselves shall be guiltless of his blood."

She vowed solemnly unto them: "Be it all according as you have said, and may the God of Israel remember me! And now," she added, "delay not a moment longer, but get you gone into the mountains and stay in hiding there at least three days. By then the men who are in pursuit of you will be wearied out and will have given up hope of finding you. Then shall you return by night by the ford, and none will molest you."

So she sent them away in safety. And they climbed down by the cord from the window that hung over the wall of the city, and fled under cover of night into the mountains. There they lay close, venturing out only after dark for food, until three days were gone by and they were out of danger of discovery. The third night they crossed the Jordan and returned into the camp at Shittim. And they reported themselves to Joshua.

"Truly," they said, "the Lord hath delivered this country into our hands. The King of Jericho and all his officers and the people that dwell in the city are faint with dread because of Israel."

They told him also of the oath they had made to the woman who had saved them from falling into the power of the King. Joshua bade them bear it continually in mind, and ensure that it was kept to the letter. He commended the two men, and was well-content with what they told him.

On the morrow the Israelites raised their camp at Shittim and marched towards the Jordan. They pitched their tents on the eastern shore of the river and remained there three days. Now it was the season of the year when the Jordan is deep in flood and overflows all its banks. It stretched out before them like a shallow sea, but deep and tumultuous in mid-stream. And there seemed to be no means whereby so great a host could cross from one side to the other, for the fords were now drowned in water, and boats they had none. But Joshua, their commander, was a man of supreme energy of mind and of a high courage. And the Lord was with him.

On the third day he sent his officers through the camp, among the people. They proclaimed that on the morrow, by the grace of God, Israel would resume the march, cross the Jordan and enter Canaan; and that they were one and all to sanctify themselves in preparation for this great day; for the Lord would do wonders. At these tidings all marvelled, and there was quiet in the camp from that hour onwards.

By sunrise on the morrow, as their Captain, Joshua, had commanded, the people had broken up their camp and were now assembled in their clans and companies and were ready. And the priests bearing the Ark of the Covenant advanced in solitude from out of the camp and continued on their way until they came to the shallow flood-waters that lay shining between them and the Jordan's usual channel. And behold, as the naked soles of the feet of the priests bearing the Ark were dipped in the brim of the water, a wondrous miracle was revealed to all that gazed. For the river that yesterday had run, swirling in flood and burdened with wreckage, in the deep gorge of the Jordan, was now dammed; its waters being heaped up near the city called Adam, above twenty miles from where Israel had been encamped.

And the priests, without pause, chanting their hymns of praise, went on down into the channel until among its boulders they were in the midst of the river's bed. There they stayed, the staves of the Ark resting on their shoulders, its gold wondrous in the sunrise. And when they had taken up their station there, the trumpets sounded. And the whole host of Israel—the men of war, the common people, the women and children, the camp-followers—went down after them with their flocks and their herds, their beasts of burden and all that they had. As they filed past the priests—none drawing near them—and looked on the Ark with its cherubim of gold, they lifted up their voices in wild acclamation, in sure trust that while this sacred emblem of Jehovah was safe in a place so full of peril, so too were they.

Hours passed by while the vast multitude of Israel moved slowly on, threading its serpentine way across the gorge. When all were safely gone their way, none hurt or injured, and not even a single lamb lost, the priests followed after them, till all were on dry land.

Then Joshua commanded that twelve picked, sturdy men, one from each of the tribes, should return into the river-bed, and bring up upon their shoulders thence twelve very hard and heavy boulders from the place where the priests had stood who bore the Ark. These Joshua set up in a circle at Gilgal, for a trophy and memorial to all that came after of the wonder that had been seen that day, so that their children's children to unnumbered generations should be continually reminded of how by the grace of God, after issuing from the wastes of the desert, they had crossed that great river, the Jordan, in safety and dry-shod.

And Israel continued the march that day and went up into the plains of Jericho, and because of this marvel the people were moved with awe and wonder and looked with fear upon Joshua even as they had feared Moses before him.

The haze-blue mountains of Moab now left behind them, they encamped in Gilgal many days and there fulfilled the rites of their religion as they were bidden by the priests. There, too, on the fourteenth day of the first month of the new year, they kept the Feast of the Passover and offered up solemn sacrifice. It was the night of the vernal full moon, as it had been in Goshen, and though in this desolate region of Gilgal little verdure is to be seen but that of the prickling briar and the thorn, and spring-time shows but thin and sparsely, yet the early flowers of the year were now in blossom, and the birds and beasts rejoiced in its sweetness. Throughout the forty years since the first Feast of the Passover had been held in Egypt never had there been such joy in Israel. It seemed almost beyond belief that the woes and hardships and the hopes so long deferred of their pilgrimage were over, and that the very soil on which they stood was the land of their desire. Here at Gilgal the host rested, while the men of war prepared to go forward to the siege of Jericho.

On the morrow after the feast, the women of Israel baked unleavened cakes of flour ground from the old corn of the last year's harvest. From that day onward the manna which had been their food in the wilderness ceased and they lived henceforward on the fruits and produce of Canaan.

Now it came to pass one day about éventide, that Joshua, having with his chief officers gone through the camp and assured himself that all was well and in order, and a strong watch posted, withdrew himself alone. He went on across the plain until, in the half light under the hills beyond it, the sombre bastions and walls of Jericho loomed into view, the last faint hues of sunset streaking the western skies. Apart from a few wild nocturnal creatures which had scurried into shelter at sound of his approach, no living thing had crossed his path.

The shades of night gathered swiftly around him as, vigilant and alone, he gazed out over the flat plain towards the mighty stronghold. The day of Israel's ordeal was at hand. And on him alone, their Captain chosen by God, its fortunes now hung. His dark clear eyes became fixed in reverie; his mind in labour with his thoughts. And as he stood musing there, the thrill as of a great peril suddenly troubled his heart. He turned abruptly, his hand on his sword-hilt, and looked. And behold, he was no longer alone, for at a few paces distant there stood as it were a man, his sword drawn in his hand. Yet his look was not like that of mortal. There dwelt a light upon his brows that was not of earth or of its skies now fading in the west; his countenance was serene and glorious. And Joshua in awe and wonder drew near and accosted him.

"Art thou", he said, "for Israel, or comest thou out armed to fight for our adversaries?"

And he said: "Nay, but as prince and captain of the host of the Lord God am I come."

Joshua doubted no more. He fell on his face to the earth, and made obeisance and worshipped. "Answer me, I beseech thee!" he cried. "What sayeth my Lord unto his servant?"

And the prince of the Lord of Hosts said to Joshua: "Loose now thy sandals from off thy feet, for the place whereon thou standest is holy."

And Joshua did so; and with all the strength of his mind he paid heed to the words the stranger uttered. Then he went his way and returned through the darkness into the camp.

Rahab had spoken truly. Rumour of the approach of Israel and of the victories they had won over the lands eastward of the Jordan had spread far and wide among the kings and chieftains and the people of Canaan. The name of Jehovah who had abased the gods of Egypt was a thing of dread to them. When then report was brought to the King of Jericho that even while the waters of the Jordan were in flood they had been gathered and heaped up as in a wall to give Israel passage, and that the whole host was now encamped at Gilgal, he was stricken with a deadly terror. There was no spirit left in him, for fear and dread of Israel. He dared not sally out to meet them.

And those that dwelt on the outskirts of the city withdrew into its shelter, bringing with them whatsoever corn and food and treasure they possessed and could carry away in haste. Its walls and battlements were manned, and the whole city was straitly shut up. None came out and none went in. Before even an enemy had showed at its gates, Jericho lay as if besieged.

And at Joshua's own time the army of Israel, men of valour, forty thousand strong, marched out from Gilgal and drew near to the city and encamped there. And the King of Jericho and his captains awaited the assault.

But day followed day, and still there showed no sign of when or how it would be delivered. Spies that were sent out under cover of darkness never returned; false alarms set the city in sudden violent uproar; and open revolt was beaten down with a cruel hand.

And in the midst of this suspense there came a day when the watchmen on Jericho's topmost turrets, as they peered out over the plain in the cheating dusk of daybreak stood aghast. A strange and terrifying spectacle met their eyes.

There debouched from out of the camp of Israel upon the plain rank upon rank of its men-at-arms, by their troops and their companies, each under its own captain, and in a great silence. Wending their way well beyond bow-shot from the walls of the city they advanced in close order, as if to encompass the whole circuit of the city. And when the men-at-arms were passed on, there followed in a space seven raimented priests bearing seven trumpets of rams' horns set in silver that were wont to be sounded on days of festival and jubilee in the tabernacle. After them, borne by four other priests upon its staves, there came an object that filled them with disquiet and boding, though they had no knowledge of its use or meaning. It was the Ark of the Covenant of the Lord. And in the rearward of the Ark, yet other thousands of armed men in close defile followed in its train.

Thus in the midst of the host went the Ark of the Lord, the priests preceding it, and, as they walked, blowing with their mouths into their clamorous trumpets of rams' horns. Else Israel marched in silence. Not a man of them spoke to his neighbour, nor made they any sound with their voices, though the clarions of the silver trumpets rang echoing clear and solemn against the walls.

The horror and mystery of the spectacle struck with a deadly cold the hearts of the king and his captains and the defenders of the city as they looked down and watched from their prodigious walls. They had never seen its like before. No wild onset of assailants shouting shrill battle-cry, no twangling storms of arrows hailing upon the walls, nor crash of battering ram. Nought but this voiceless multitude of gaunt and fearless tribesmen, sun-scorched and lean with long travail in the thirsty wilds of the desert, marching on and on in a hush broken only by the shuffle of their footsteps in the sands and the sudden horrific rending of the air by blasts of the silver trumpets of their priests. And after the priests, this gold-slabbed coffer—its bearers clad in strange embroidered vestments—awful emblem of Jehovah, the unseen and unimaginable foe. This and this only. For when the city had thus been compassed once about, the army of Israel withdrew into its camp.

Thus at daybreak for six days one after another the whole host of the army of Israel made the circuit of Jericho; and to those who manned its walls, wearied out with the last watch of night, it was as though the city were an island girt about and encircled with a slow-moving river, not of waters but of men. They were besieged with fear, fear of these

[242]

enemies without and of the fate awaiting them, and fear of the horror of the mystery in their imaginations.

The seventh day dawned, clear and cloudless in the spring of the year, and yet again the city was encompassed round about as it had been hitherto, but in the mien of those who made the circuit of the city there had come a change. They trod as if exultant, and speechless with joy. And when this day the full circuiting was completed there rang from out of the trumpets of the priests a shrilling clarion, wilder and longer than any that had sounded yet. And when the echo of this clangour ceased, the whole host of Israel suddenly shouted together with a great and mighty shout. And lo, when the sound of the trumpets and of this mighty shout had ceased, it came to pass that the walls of Jericho were broken and fell down flat, its gates were flung open, and the army of Israel went in, every man straight before him. They took the city by storm, burned it with fire, and destroyed all that were within it, except only the woman Rahab, her father and mother and her household, as had been sworn to her by the spies.

From conquest on to conquest under Joshua the armies of Israel marched on. In the first few years that followed the fall of Jericho, of the kings and chieftains whom he met in battle and who warred either in their own might in defence of their cities, or banded themselves together in alliance under one among them greater than they, he vanquished thirty-one.

But centuries were yet to pass before the nations in Canaan were finally subdued. And though the land was divided by Joshua between the tribes each within its own boundaries, according to its strength and numbers, they were not only repeatedly at war with their enemies, but in strife one with another. The day was yet far distant when